Mark McKnight hails from Northern Ireland although there have been complaints filed that he doesn't get back there often enough. He has lived in 23 houses, owned 5 sofas and played in 4 bands. He has no wife or children but hopes to remedy that at some point. He is probably on facebook right now.

More Village At The End Of The World Stories (henceforth known as 'M.V.A.T.E.O.T.W.S.') is the second instalment in this four part epic and is arguably his greatest work to date. All that is needed is for Mark to die young and have a real author complete the set.

'M.V.A.T.E.O.T.W.S.' is his seventh printed work.

Forthcoming & Already Available Titles
By Mark McKnight

Msimulizi: Stories For Mwangaza
Msimulizi 2: The Green Dragon
Msimulizi 3: Get Out Of My House!
Msimulizi 4: As Yet Untitled

The Village At The End Of The World
More Village At The End Of The World Stories
The Village At The Other End Of The World
The End Of The World At The Village At The End Of The
World

500: A Collection Of Very Short Stories
501: A Collection Of Slightly Longer Stories

Tales From Africa

On The Road

more village at the end of the world stories

mark mcknight

Baby
Mosquito
Books

ISBN 978-1-905691-06-7

Printed and bound in Great Britain and the United States by
Lightning Source Inc.

Mark McKnight
189 Pendleton Road
Darlington
DL1 2EP
ENGLAND

http://www.babymosquito.com
mark@babymosquito.com

In Memory Of Carole

And For Pete
Again, Damnit!
I don't understand why.

Contents

more village at the end of the world stories

mark mcknight

mark mcknight

preface

The Village At The End Of The World was inspired by
Gaba, a village in Uganda, East Africa. It is literally at
the end of the road, when you can go no further, except
into Lake Victoria. Of course, in the Village At The End
Of The World, things don't always happen the way they
do in the real world. Please enjoy these stories inspired
by my travels around the world and the people and
things I have seen.

babies, babies, babies

Wednesday, February 1st

Following the enormous success and rave reviews of their musical, 'The Heifer and The Fiddle Player,' the Village At The End Of the World Amateur Dramatic Society will be auditioning for their forthcoming Nativity Play. All parts are open to permanent residents of the Village At The End Of The World. Mary and Joseph must be human, everything else is fair game. The part of Baby Jesus will be cast exactly ten months from today in time for the performance. Rehearsals begin this and every Tuesday at 6:37pm sharp in the church hall.

That was the notice that found it's way to the
notice board outside the mayor, Mr. Hubert Q. Lion's
office. When the V.A.T.E.O.T.W.A.D.S. (Village At The End
Of The World Amateur Dramatic Society) first
approached the mayor with their idea of a nativity play
on an outdoor stage in the middle of the village green,
Mr. Hubert Q. Lion was sceptical. However, Cyril and
Bob (long time residents of the village) were rather
persuasive. They assured the doubtful lion that it
would be a fantastic civic occasion and that it would all
take place with the minimum of fuss to the village as a
whole.

It was as a result of this discussion that the notice
was posted and preparations began for what was to
become the source of many a joke, story and song. Yet
Mr. Hubert Q. Lion somehow couldn't shake the picture
of a snowball teetering at the top of a mountain, ready
to begin its catastrophic descent.

On the following Tuesday, the entire village was
already at the church hall waiting for the auditions to
begin. By now a teenager, Chihuahua was there with
her whole family: mother (Victoria), father (Baz),
grandmother and Cyril the cartographer although no-
one was yet quite sure how he was related to
the others. Bob and Joy were there holding
hands and whispering sweet nothings as

Wilson (Joy's father and the deputy mayor) twiddled with the pointed ends of his mustache. The symphony orchestra that was in town had shown up, except for the Violinists' Dairy Co-Operative who showed up late once they had finished the milking. The whole police force were there: Grandpa, Big Rab, Lonely Jake, The Leaf and Fred. They milled around picking fleas off one another and trying to find some bananas. Monkeys can be *so* unrefined!

It seemed like everyone was speaking at once, pronouncing which part they felt best suited to and making their predictions about who might be cast as which other parts. The hubbub of noise in the room was invigorating. Everyone was imagining themselves on the stage delivering their lines as if they were Hamlet or Macbeth or something. Some of them were having a little practice of the lines they had prepared. For the auditions, each person had been asked to prepare a short speech of what they thought the wise men might have said to Mary and Joseph when they arrived at the stable on that first Christmas so many years ago.

At 6:37pm precisely, the doors to the church hall burst open and in strode Pete and Deaf Al. Pete had, until recently, been the caretaker of the Land of the Windmills but he had tricked the two symphony orchestras into taking over his job on a rotating basis.

Deaf Al really was deaf: it wasn't just a nickname. He was a bellmaker and had become deaf from testing the bells that he made. He wore a hearing aid but it doesn't inspire you with confidence when your musical director doesn't hear most of what is said, never mind sung.

Of the two, Deaf Al was by far the more intense. In his arms he carried a wide variety of papers, boxes and of course his briefcase. From the moment the doors burst open, he was talking. Talking to those who wanted to audition, talking to those who didn't but mostly talking to Pete. He took long strides and sat down by the piano, announced 'OK daaarlings, let's hear how you can sing.' He began to thump out a well known melody on the 'ivories' and encouraged everyone present to join in.

Pete, for his part, shuffled into the room after Deaf Al had begun his sing-song. Holding a flat cap in his hands, he did not seem to be the inspirational director that the rest of the village was hoping for.

As quickly as Deaf Al had begun the singing, he brought it to a close. 'Fine daaarlings. Now you're warmed up, let's get right along with the auditions,' he said. He issued a few more directions and soon he and Pete were installed at a desk auditioning people one by one to decide who would be cast in which part for their nativity play.

By 10:26pm exactly, they had listened to one hundred and thirty seven different ideas of what the wise men said to baby Jesus when they arrived at the stable and they were ready to make their decision. Pete got up to speak this time, politely thanking everyone for their hard work. The parts list would be posted outside the village hall first thing in the morning. Pete and Deaf Al deliberated long into the night, trying to decide between so many wonderful and a few not so wonderful actors and actresses.

There was a crowd outside the village hall from first light the next morning: everyone was desperate to know how they had been cast. A heavy air of anticipation was in the air as Pete carefully and deliberately tacked the second notice over the top of the first one.

Village At The End Of The World
Nativity Play
Cast List

Mary & Joseph: Joy & Bob
Baby Jesus: TBA
Wise Men: Cyril, Baz, Wilson
Shepherds: V.A.T.E.O.T.W.P.D.
Innkeeper: Chihuahua
Donkey: Mr. Hubert Q. Lion

Music: The Village At The End Of The World
        Symphony Orchestras

Costumes: Chihuahua's mum & Grandma
Props: The men who play the big drums
Lighting: The Violinists' Dairy Co-Operative

Reminder:

Rehearsals are every Tuesday at 6:37pm sharp in
the church hall.

And so the rehearsals began in earnest. Although it was still only the fourteenth of February, this was such a complicated nativity play that they needed all the time they could find to be ready by December 25th. There was just one thing that nobody understood. They had never heard of this person 'TBA' that had been cast as the Baby Jesus. It was Chihuahua who finally plucked up the courage to ask Deaf Al what it all meant. Deaf Al laughed and laughed when she asked. Between fits of giggles, he explained that TBA was short for 'To Be Announced.' There was no point in casting a Baby Jesus now: the baby would be almost one year old by the time the play came around. Since the baby didn't need to learn any lines, it was much better to wait for a baby who was born later in the year to be their Baby Jesus. All he would have to do was lie in the manger and hopefully not cry but you could never be too sure with babies.

This news spread through the village like wildfire. Everyone knew that it was a great honour, and possibly good luck for life, for a baby to be cast as the Baby Jesus. It was because of this that each person in the Village At The End Of The World, including the monkeys had the same idea at more or less the same time: 'What if it was my baby that was the Baby Jesus.'

Now in the Village At The End Of The World, they

did not go through the usual method of getting babies (with the stork and the basket and the chimney and everything). They had refined the process to a series of application forms. As long as you filled in the proper forms, enclosed two passport size photographs and enclosed the correct fee, in nine months you could drop by the very same office in the back of the village hall where you dropped the forms off and pick up your brand new baby.

Not many people had been back to that particular office before. Nobody had really wanted a new baby in the Village At The End Of The World and besides, there were other more fun things to do if you wanted a baby. During the month of February, the baby office was inundated with requests for forms. Princess Lydia, who had just begun working there, had to travel to the Big City three times in a month to get more copies of the baby forms.

The first form (or the B-1) was the easy one. Here's a copy I found lying around after the rush:

Village At The End Of The World
Baby Application Form
Form B-1

Name: _____

Age: _____

Do you want a baby?   **Yes/No**

Are you sure?   **Yes/No**

You know they're noisy and stink? **Yes/No**

Do you want a boy or girl?   **Boy/Girl**

Have you any experience   **Yes/No**
    with babies?

If no, have you ever been   **Yes/No**
    a baby yourself?

Signed: _____

Date: _____

As you can see, getting a baby wasn't exactly the most difficult thing in the world but fortunately, the second form (the B-2) was the one where many prospective parents fell down. It was part general knowledge exam about babies and part shock tactics to scare away only the most serious of applicants.

Village At The End Of The World
Baby Application Form
Form B-2

Name: _____

Could you spell that
       please?   _____

What colour is a baby? _____

Which smells more, a
       baby or a pig?   **Baby/Pig**

What do babies eat?   _____

Do you know about baby poo?
**Well let me tell you, there's a whole lot
of it from just one baby.**

What about baby wee wee?
Lot's of that too. Better get used to it.

Babies throw up regularly.
**That's not a question. We're just
warning you.**

Signed: _____

Date: _____

Finally, the B-3 form was really only a formality
although for obvious reasons it was essential.

Village At The End Of The World
Baby Application Form
Form B-3

Name: _____

Species: **Human / Monkey**
            Aquatic (eg. Fish) / Bird
            Other (Please Specify)

            _____

Signed: _____

Date: _____

And that was it. Three forms, two passport size photographs and the application fee and you were ready to receive your baby in precisely nine months. Of course, as with all local administrations, your application could be delayed or refused for any one of a number of minor offences: a misspelled word, a different date on different forms or even if it was a Friday afternoon and the official couldn't be bothered processing your forms until Monday.

As the months were ripped off the calendars around the Village At The End Of The World, you could positively feel the anticipation building around the village. In all, seventy five separate applications had been made at the baby office and only two of those had been rejected, both from the men who play the big drums who thought they were applying for a 'lady.' They got quite a shock when Princess Lydia explained that it was the 'Baby Office' and not the 'Lady Office.'

December 1st soon rolled around and the Village At The End Of The World was alive with the screams of seventy three newborn babies. Rehearsals for the nativity play had been going rather well although with the babies, things had almost ground to a standstill. That evening, at 6:37pm on the dot, Deaf Al burst through the door with his usual flamboyancy and Pete followed soon after, nodding and agreeing with everything that Deaf Al pronounced forth. However, as he came through the doors to the church hall, one hundred and forty six (two for each baby) parents put their fingers to their lips and said, 'Sssssshhhh!!!'

The rest of the evening was spent admiring babies. Of course, Deaf Al and Pete were careful to coo over each one and say, 'Awwww!!!' at all the right times. When they had viewed about half of the babies, Pete caught Deaf Al's eyes and shared a look that communicated everything that needed to be said. Pete took meticulous notes on each baby and once all the parents and babies

had departed, they sat down to discuss which baby
might be cast as the Baby Jesus.

Not a word needed to be said: they were in the
midst of a crisis that neither of them knew how to or
had the guts to solve. Each and every parent was
convinced that their child was the cutest and therefore
should be cast as the baby Jesus. The problem was that
to pick one child meant a hundred and sixty four irate
parents. Neither man had the heart to tell any one
parent that their child couldn't be the baby Jesus and so
they settled on a plan that was so daft, it just might
work.

With three more weeks of rehearsal, the nativity
play was ready to go. Christmas Eve was spent putting
the final touches. All the actors tried on the costumes
that had been tailor made for them by Chihuahua's
mother, grandmother and Princess Lydia. The men who
played the big drums had excelled themselves with the
props and the set design. It truly looked like a hot and
dusty afternoon in first century Israel as you looked at
the stage, even though it was really a bitterly cold
Winter's evening in the Village At The End Of The
World. The Violinists' Dairy Co-Operative busied
themselves making sure all of their lights were working
and properly protected against the elements.

Christmas Day began the way it always does:

blueberry pancakes for breakfast, church, a huge
dinner and a long, lazy nap. However, as five o' clock
rolled around, the village began to awake and assemble
by the open stage on the village green. Word had spread
far and wide about the nativity play and the audience
was quite substantial, especially for Christmas Night.
As the play began, still nobody knew which baby was to
be the Baby Jesus.

As Mary and Joseph arrived at the inn, the
innkeeper told them he had no room. In fact,
Chihuahua (as the innkeeper) showed Bob and Joy
(Joseph and Mary) that she really had no room: the inn
was filled up with seventy three babies who were all
sucking on fresh bottles. So Mary and Joseph were
forced to sleep in the stable.

The first act closed just as Mary and Joseph were
settling down for the night in the stable. Audience and
cast alike were on tenterhooks, waiting to find out
which baby would be the Baby Jesus. The interval
seemed interminable: it was only fifteen minutes but it
seemed like a lifetime as people stretched their legs,
bought a hot cup of tea or went to spend a penny.

Just before the curtains opened for the second half
of the play, it began to snow. As the orchestra
began their entr'acte, seventy three parents
were certain that their child would be

the one. However, as the curtains opened and the lights faded in, a collective gasp went up from everyone. There in the manger, dressed in a nappy replete with dummy was Deaf Al. He had cast himself as the Baby Jesus.

When Cyril, Baz and Wilson (the three wise men) arrived on the scene, they couldn't get their lines out because they were laughing so much. Things went from bad to worse: next on the scene were the shepherds. Monkeys can be unstable at the best of times but this was too much and the whole play degenerated into a fit of giggles.

Somehow, the cast muddled through to the end of the performance. The audience loved it. They thought it was a fantastic idea, casting an adult as the Baby Jesus. The loved it so much, they gave the cast a standing ovation. The applause and cheering lasted for a long, long time.

A few days later, when things had settled back to normal again, Mr. Hubert Q. Lion got a letter from a very important source.

Dear Mr. Hubert Q. Lion,

Let me congratulate on your triumph of a nativity play this Christmas Night. I haven't laughed so hard since my mother-in-law had a cake thrown in her face. I hope this will be the first annual Village At The End Of The World nativity play? I look forward to next year's offering with baited breath. I'm sure those seventy three newborns you had in the inn will certainly add to the performance as one-year-olds.

Yours sincerely,
Baron Friedrich von
Hoffenbausenfurgenblitzenkirschfleigemen-
jurgenflurgenmurgenwurgensen

Mr. Hubert Q. Lion sent for Pete and Weird Al and made them promise that next year they would outdo themselves, producing a nativity play that was even better. They began rehearsals right away.

the orchard

On a beautiful Summer afternoon, with the sun blazing down from a deep blue sky without a single cloud, Bob and Joy were casually wandering along the beach and dipping their toes in the water when Bob came across something that he really didn't expect to find there on the beach. At first, he thought there must be some mistake. It was a thing that he hadn't seen for long years, since he had left the Big City in search of Joy. Yet there at his feet, as plain as day lay something that Bob assumed he would never eat again. It was a rosy red apple. Only shiny green apples had been seen in the Village At The End Of The World ever since anyone could remember.

Always with an eye for the suspicious and strange events that could lead to crisis, Princess Joy suggested that they take the apple to her father, the deputy mayor. He would know what to do. Bob, on the other hand had a much more pleasant suggestion. They could share this apple and take the other one that was further on up the beach to Wilson. Joy countered with an even better suggestion. Bob could eat the first apple, Joy would eat the second and they would take the third apple that Joy had found to her father.

As they looked all along the beach, they found a total of thirteen apples spread up and down the beach. As they munched on the two that they had held back for themselves, they collected the others to take them to Wilson to see what the deputy mayor thought of this interesting development.

As the eleven shiny red apples sat in a little pile on the deputy mayor's desk, Wilson and Mr. Hubert Q. Lion scratched their heads and perused what exactly might be the meaning of this particular development. Yet the more they thought about it, the less they could work out where these apples might have come from.

As the days continued to pass, more and more apples began to wash up on the beach. The residents of the village were thankful for these shiny red apples but few stopped to think what the meaning of this 'drift-fruit' might be. Those who did ponder it remained unsure as to what it all meant.

Soon, supply outstripped demand and there were more apples washing up on the beach than the people

of the village could managed to consume. All the
storerooms were filled with shiny red apples and the
ants were loving all the extra food they were getting for
free.

A few days later, as Bob and Joy were having a
picnic on the beach (a picnic of shiny red apples), they
saw the strangest of things coming over the horizon. It
looked like the top of some trees but from a distance, it
was difficult to see. Within the space of seven minutes
and fourteen seconds, the entire village was assembled
on the beach, watching to find out what exactly this was
that was approaching the village.

As whatever this was that was approaching got a
little larger, the colour of the trees made it certain that
this is where the apples had been coming from. These
had to be apple trees in full blossom. Yet as this orchard
on the ocean drifted towards the shore, the current
changed the direction and whatever it was started to
drift sideways instead of towards the beach.

The 10 Commandments of the Village At The End
Of The World were posted on signposts at regular
intervals along the beach:

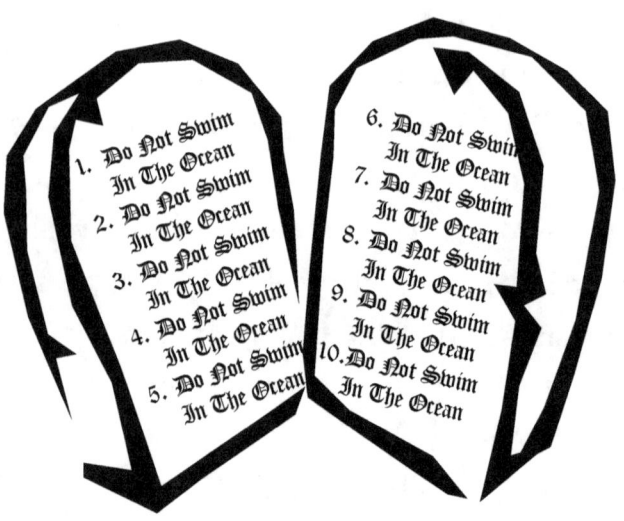

1. Do Not Swim In The Ocean
2. Do Not Swim In The Ocean
3. Do Not Swim In The Ocean
4. Do Not Swim In The Ocean
5. Do Not Swim In The Ocean
6. Do Not Swim In The Ocean
7. Do Not Swim In The Ocean
8. Do Not Swim In The Ocean
9. Do Not Swim In The Ocean
10. Do Not Swim In The Ocean

As such, only two people had ever swam in the ocean. On the first day Mr. Hubert Q. Lion had arrived in the village, he had chased Chihuahua in to the ocean and they had almost fallen over the edge of a strange waterfall that was in the middle of the ocean. Whatever this was that was drifting in the ocean was heading straight towards the waterfall. Mr. Hubert Q. Lion in particular had been especially fond of the rosy red apples that had washed up on the beach. He alone (for Chihuahua had only been a baby at the time) knew that these rosy red apples would soon come to an end if the mysterious orchard was allowed to drift over the waterfall, whether it was truly the end of the world or not.

An emergency rescue mission was what was

necessary. Somebody, somehow had to go and rescue this orchard so that the village could have their apples. The island was drifting very slowly so it was clear that they still had a couple of days before the apples were gone for good. The problem was that nobody could be found to mount a rescue operation. After all, who would risk their own life purely for some apples.

The next morning, as a couple of violinists were having a breakfast of apples on the beach, they saw something quite remarkable. The floating orchard had drifted close enough to be able to make out the individual trees. There, waving a flag and shouting for help were two girls. All of a sudden , there was a whole host of volunteers to help these unknown girls. People were willing to sacrifice the apples to save their own bacon. Nobody wanted to let two innocent girls die by drifting over the end of the world.

By lunch time, a whole flotilla of rafts, boats and sailing dinghies had been constructed by every spare set of hands who could help rescue these two girls. Like an armada, the Village At The End Of The World Navy set off in their hastily constructed crafts to rescue two girls and (of course) the apples. In less than an hour, the wide variety of ocean going vessels had beached on the shore of what appeared to be a floating island. Fiona and Sania, the two girls who had been screaming for help from the island were overjoyed that their rescuers had come. However, when they explained their story, it was even more bizarre than the appearance of this island.

Fiona and Sania had been the the orchard keepers of an orchard that was right on the shore of a huge lake. The apples were widely recognised as the best, rosiest, shiniest, reddest apples in the whole of the world. The ground was so good that no weeds grew there. It was so soft that when the apples fell off the trees, they didn't bruise at all. The orchard had such a gentle slope that when the apples fell off the trees, they slowly rolled along to one end of the vineyard. All that Fiona and Sania had to do was to change the barrels every day and put the full barrels on the back of the truck to take it to market.

As a result, the two girls would spend their days lazing around the vineyard. Often they would lie sleeping on the soft earth in the comfortable shade of the apple blossoms. They would enjoy their days, talking and singing in the afternoon sunshine.

One day, disaster had struck. Fiona and Sania had been napping peacefully after changing the barrels in the morning. Before they knew what was happening, an earthquake had very gently shaken the orchard. Not enough to waken Fiona and Sania, but enough to shake lose the orchard from the mainland. As the two girls remained sleeping in the soft, cool shade of an apple tree, the orchard changed from a peninsula in a lake to a floating island on a lake. The island then drifted across the lake, onto a river that emptied out of the lake and before long was floating out to sea.

When they had woken up, Fiona and Sania had panicked. Yet somehow they had managed to survive for six months with nothing to eat apart from the apples that they were growing. They had drifted endlessly and had almost given up hope. Mostly, they had been drifting so far out to sea that they couldn't even see the land. Finally, a couple of days ago, they had come close enough to land to see people watching them. That was when they had made flag out of an old pair of shorts and a branch from a tree. That was also when the people in the village had decided to mount their rescue operation.

After an impromptu village meeting, the people of the Village At The End Of The World had decided what they would do. Fiona and Sania were evacuated right away. While an apple a day is rumoured to keep the doctor away, nothing but apples is surely not very good for you. Pete carried the two girls back to land on his raft made of tree branches and banana fibres. Arriving on dry

land for the first time in months, the girls were ecstatic.
They were even happier when Princess Lydia produced
some real food: potatoes, roast beef, vegetables and
bread. However, their faces fell when Princess Lydia
offered them some apple juice to drink. The princess
did offer them the alternative of mango juice which
both Fiona and Sania gratefully accepted.

With the two girls safely ashore, the villagers
began their work on the island. Pete furiously rowed
his raft back to the island, this time weighed down by
ropes, chains and string. Pete arrived back on the island
just before dark. Nobody wanted to be out on open
water after dark so they decided that, since the island
was drifting so slowly, they could wait until morning to
begin work.

At the first light of dawn, the whole village began
working as if their lives depended on it. In fact, their
lives did depend on it. If they couldn't rescue the
floating orchard, they and the island would fall off the
end of the world: no more people, no more island and
no more apples. Every man, woman and child began
attaching the ropes; one end to a tree on the island and
the other end to their boats, rafts and dinghies.

By just before lunch, they were ready for their last
ditch effort. Before they went, everyone gorged
themselves on apples. This might be the last chance

they got to eat these most wonderful of apples before they were gone for good over the edge of the world.

With everyone's bellies full, they launched the ships once again, this time attached to the island. Grabbing the oars that they had made, everyone began furiously rowing towards the shore. The great weight of the island was almost too much. No matter how they strained, it was as if the island wouldn't move. As they gradually wore themselves out from their efforts, they felt the whole island shift, ever so slightly. The current had changed ever so gently in their direction. As the people continued to row, it picked up speed and not a moment too soon, it began to float gently in the direction of the shore, for already people could hear the thundering roar of the huge waterfall.

By the middle of the afternoon, they were out of danger and by dinnertime, the island was firmly back to the shore and had been anchored with sturdy ropes so that it didn't drift away again. Fiona and Sania were so happy that the island had been saved. Now that they were safe and had a good meal, they had been beside themselves with worry over what might happen to their precious orchard of apples.

After lengthy discussions, the mayor decided what must be done next. Since there was no possibility of the orchard ever being returned to its rightful owners, it would remain tethered to the beach beside the Village At The End Of The World. Fiona and Sania would remain as its keepers and would use their apples to trade with the rest of the village. Once again, the orchard began producing the rosiest, shiniest, reddest apples in the whole world.

And nobody ever did find out whether the waterfall really marked the end of the world or not.

dipped

As is the case in a great many stories concerning the Village At The End Of The World, this particular story begins with the arrival of a solitary figure along the Village At The End Of The World Highway.

This particular individual was what one might describe as 'dapper.' He wore an immaculate black pinstripe suit: carefully pleated trousers, a morning jacket and three buttoned waistcoat. The ensemble was complemented by a spotless white shirt with yellow and gold tie, tied with the classic Windsor knot. Gold cuff links inlaid with what looked like diamonds sparkled in the morning sunshine and the sheen from his lovingly polished black shoes neatly rounded off the whole outfit. In his hand, he casually swung a calfskin leather briefcase that was clearly almost empty by the way it elegantly swung at his side.

Stopping just once for directions, Mr. Jonathan Campbell-Smythe made his way to the mayor's office to

present his credentials and explain why he was there.
Mr. Hubert Q. Lion wasn't around so Wilson, the deputy
mayor, entertained this impeccably dressed visitor in
the mayor's parlour. The conversation eventually got
around to the purpose of Mr. Jonathan Campbell-
Smythe's visit. He was, according to his letter of
introduction, a very important official of the Big City
Ministry of Agriculture, Livestock, Farming and
Fisheries.

In a very prim and proper voice, Mr. Jonathan
Campbell-Smythe explained that a very strange
sickness was sweeping the land, affecting all kinds of
animals. Mostly, this strange disease affected farm
animals, cows in particular, but it could afflict any type
of animal from the tiniest ant up to the mightiest
elephant.

Snoring Sickness had first appeared in a village on
the other side of the Big City, but it had quickly spread
throughout the countryside, afflicting sheep, cows, pigs,
donkeys, horses, chickens, dogs, cats and a whole host of
other species. For some reason, it didn't do anything to
human beings, but all other animals were vulnerable to
this most strange illness. Like the name suggests,
this malady made the animals who were
infected snore uncontrollably. It didn't
affect their eggs or wool or milk or

meat or anything else: it simply meant that the farmers didn't get any sleep because their animals were all snoring. Worse still, when an animal fell asleep with Snoring Sickness, it could be up to three days before they woke up again.

Some rather smart boffins in the Big City had put their collective minds together and within a few days had managed to come up with a remarkable cure for this disease. It even worked in advance: if an animal was treated before the disease, it worked just like an immunisation. Like the injections that the mean old doctors used to give us in the bum when we were just little!

To cut a long story short, the government had decided that they would strike before things got out of hand. They had introduced a programme to inoculate every domestic animal in the whole world; from one end to the other. Mr. Jonathan Campbell-Smythe was here to ensure that every animal in the Village At The End Of The World was treated. The treatment was really quite simple. A huge bath was filled to the brim with the foul smelling, dark brown liquid that was the treatment. It had to be huge, because each animal had to be completely submerged in the evil smelling fluid. If even a square inch was missed, the treatment might not work.

Without any hesitation, Wilson agreed that they should begin work right away. He would personally help Mr. Jonathan Campbell-Smythe to oversee the project. A work party of off duty musicians was soon organised to construct the bath. They set about their task eagerly, intrigued as to the use of this most odd bath they were building. Although it was rather too large for a person, there was a crisis when a representative from the Violinists' Dairy Co-Operative arrived and explained that the bath (which was almost completed) was not large enough for their largest cows.

Leaving their first bath unfinished, they set work on building their second bath, with just a little less enthusiasm than the first attempt. Wilson circled the bath scratching his head. The larger bath would certainly not be a problem. The problem that was in his head was the ants. Mr. C-S had been very specific: every animal that lived in the village and its surroundings had to be treated. If the ants went into this bath, they would surely drown. Once the musicians had finished building the second bath, they constructed a third, ant-sized, bath for treating the ants against Snoring Sickness.

As Grandpa arrived on the scene, the musicians waited for the next bad news. It hadn't taken long for the monkeys to hear about what was happening and he had come to find out what exactly was going on. Grandpa was accompanied by his entire police force: Fred, Big Rab, Lonely Jake and The Leaf. When Wilson delicately explained the situation, Grandpa was furious. He wasn't particularly concerned about being treated for Snoring Sickness. As a matter of fact, he was quite looking forward to some free medical treatment and a bit of a swim. The problem was that they had to share the same bath as the cows owned by the Violinists' Dairy Co-Operative. They were quite simply not going to do any such of a thing. They were policemen and should be treated with all the respect that such a job commands.

Wilson managed to convince the musicians to complete the fourth bath, although with much less gusto than when they built the first. As they were finishing and Wilson was about to send them home, a thought suddenly hit him. The musicians were ordered back to work to construct a fifth bath although this time it was with a certain amount of reluctance as they all wanted to get home to their families.

Mr. Jonathan Campbell-Smythe conducted his final quality control check before he allowed the musicians to go home. Although he ignored the first bath and was a little concerned about the fifth, he felt that two, three and four were acceptable and since

Wilson was reluctant to explain what the final bath was for, Mr. C-S was happy enough. Treatment would begin at dawn the following day. All animals were expected to attend and be treated and as many humans as could be mustered were needed to help with the treatment.

With the first rays of sun, Mr. Jonathan Campbell-Smythe was to be found explaining to his volunteers how the process actually worked. The animals would jump into the bath at one end. While they were in the bath, they had to be pushed right under the waving, gurgling liquid. This was accomplished with the help of a big stick. It wasn't exactly graceful or pleasant but it was the only way to do it. Once they had been right under, the treatment was complete. The next man in line (or the next two or three) had to use a big hook to pull the animal back from under the water, along to the end of the bath where the animal could climb up the sturdily constructed steps to safety. Once the process was complete, they could begin work on the next animal. If, however, the animal being treated was a dog, it was good advice to stand well back before starting again if one wanted to avoid being covered in the stinky medicine as the dog shook its coat.

By breakfast time, the baths had been filled with the treatment that smelled like a cross between toothpaste and dirty nappies. The moment the baths were ready, all five monkeys jumped into their bath at once, enjoying this moment of fun before they had to get back to the serious business of police work. Wilson let them enjoy themselves for a while, splashing about in the dark brown, putrid smelling substance but then explained that they must be treated properly, one by one. That's exactly what happened, although not one of the monkeys was impressed when they were dunked under water with a big stick.

With the monkeys taken care of and dispatched, Wilson and Mr. Jonathan Campbell-Smythe were able to turn their attention to the two long lines that were waiting by the second and third baths. The ants were marching one by one into their bath, under the water and up the steps at the far end. It was clear that there were to be no problems with the ants in their treatment against Snoring Sickness. Anyway, one ant with Snoring Sickness wouldn't be much to worry about since it would be so quiet but a whole colony (with several billion ants) would be loud enough to keep the whole village awake.

Wilson and Mr. Jonathan Campbell-Smythe both turned at the same time to the source of a rather loud noise that was most disconcerting. As they looked along the line of cows waiting for their treatment (and ably herded by a platoon of violinists), they saw that one cow had fallen asleep. The noise it was making was worse than listening to a freight train go past. This cow had clearly contracted the dreaded Sleeping Sickness.

From somewhere, the volunteers found a new vigour in treating the cows. They didn't want to listen to any more cows falling asleep as they waited in the line. Yet no matter how hard they worked, they couldn't seem to keep up: cows were falling asleep all over the place. A company of violinists swarmed around trying to wake the cows up with only limited success.

Finally, by mid afternoon, all of the cows in the village had been woken up and treated. The V.D.C. (Violinists' Dairy Co-Operative) were full of thanks and praise for the sterling work that Wilson, Mr. Jonathan Campbell-Smythe and their team had done. With a final farewell, they began herding their cows back out onto the green pastures with the lush grass that made their milk the best in the world.

As Mr. Jonathan Campbell-Smythe was gathering his papers into his briefcase and preparing to leave, Wilson ordered the musicians to fill the fifth bath. Everyone looked at each other in confusion but just two words from Wilson made everyone run away so that only he and Mr. C-S were left standing by the fourth bath: "The mayor!" Nobody was brave enough to push Mr. Hubert Q. Lion into the foul, brown liquid so they all promptly disappeared.

Wilson quickly found the men who play the big drums, well known for their brute force and their dislike for the mayor. When he explained what was happening (they had been off enjoying a cold soda while all the dipping had been going on), they were only too happy to help. It would be their pleasure to push the mayor into the bath.

As the two men arrived at Mr. Hubert Q. Lion's house, they discovered something very worrying indeed. Both the mayor and his wife had clearly been infected with Snoring Sickness because the monumental noise coming from their bedroom window was deafening. This was clearly a job for more than two men. With cajoling and persuading, they managed to convince the rest of the percussion section to help them. They began by carrying Princess Lydia's bed, with her still sleeping in it out to the village green where the fourth bath was ready and waiting.

Princess Lydia was unceremoniously tipped into the medicine and she awoke instantly. Her roars could be heard from as far away as the Land Of The Windmills but since Mr. Hubert Q. Lion was not simply sleeping but was infected with Snoring Sickness, he was not woken by the sound of the roars. Fortunately, Wilson was able to explain to Princess Lydia what was going on and why they had kidnapped (should that be lion-napped?) her from her house and thrown her into the foul smelling bath.

Buoyed by the success of their first lion treatment, the percussion section returned to the Lion household and prepared to treat Mr. Hubert Q. Lion in a similar manner. The operation went like clockwork until the moment when the mayor rolled off his comfortable bed and into the specially prepared bath. The moment he hit the water, Mr. Hubert Q. Lion awoke and was furious. He had been sleeping since before Mr. Jonathan Campbell-Smythe had arrived in the village. From his position, someone had thrown him into a bath of the most rancid liquid for no reason. And he would not stop roaring.

Wilson knew that they only had one chance to treat the mayor because once he was out, he was never going to go back in to the bath. The whole percussion section stood around the sides of the bath, trying to push Mr. Hubert Q. Lion under with big sticks. The mayor was not so easily dipped as the rest of the animals. He squirmed and fought, twisted and turned, determined not to let the men who played the big drums defeat him.

Yet just as he was about to climb out the steps at the end without having been right under the liquid, Princess Lydia Lion let out a huge roar, jumped high in the air and landed on top of her husband, pushing both herself and the struggling male lion underneath. Everyone jumped back as the medicine slopped over the side of the bath. With all kinds of furious roars, Mr. Hubert Q. Lion broke the surface and jumped out of the bath, right over the side without using the steps.

As he stood growling with fury in his eyes and the horrible brown liquid dripping from his mane, Princess Lydia looked at her husband with tender eyes and managed to calm him down enough to explain the whole business about the Snoring Sickness. When the princess had finished explaining, Mr. Hubert Q. Lion congratulated his deputy mayor on a job well done.

Mr. Jonathan Campbell-Smythe shook the hands of Wilson and Mr. Hubert Q. Lion and went on his merry way, back along the Village At The End Of The World Highway towards the next village that had to be treated for Snoring Sickness. Wilson marvelled at how his pin stripe suit, his shiny leather shoes and his golden tie were still as immaculate as the moment he arrived in the village. The only sign that told the tale of what had happened was a tiny splash of the evil smelling brown liquid that had fallen on his collar.

the sunshine fairy

Looking back on childhood summers, the weeks stretched out longer than the ropes that held the apple orchard in place and the sun split the sky for days on end. That is how I remember my summers, and I'm sure you do too. Days were filled playing childhood games and drinking cold lemonade in the afternoon sunshine.

Yet in the Village At The End Of The World, life was really like that. Despite being at the very edge of the ocean, the village seemed to have remarkably good weather. Of course, it rained occasionally, but it was that misty rain that is oh so enjoyable in which to go walking. There were never any of the squalls, storms or tempests that raged in off the sea in the village where I grew up. Living by the ocean there was a constant battle against the wind and the rain. We used to have a saying: If you can see the lighthouse, it's going to rain. If you can't see the lighthouse, it's already raining!

For some reason, the Village At The End Of The World wasn't like that. It was like an endless summer where people had garden parties, wore summer dresses and stopped for ice lollies whenever they had the tiniest excuse to do so. Breakfast, lunch *and* dinner were all eaten outside and there weren't even any flies or wasps to disturb you while you were eating. Without a doubt, the climate in the Village At The End Of The World was one of the most pleasant in the whole world.

Unlike many other stories from this particular village, the problem was not caused by someone arriving along the Village At The End Of The World Highway. As a matter of fact, there was really nothing that happened that began the great rainstorm of '82. More worryingly still, there was nothing that anybody could have done to prevent it but that is by the by.

One afternoon, as many of the residents were having their afternoon nap, a soft rain began to fall in the village. Few people stirred from their siestas. A few cats moved from sleeping on the porch to sleeping inside the house in front of the fire, but aside from that, little was different than any other little shower of rain. By dinnertime, however, the rain had not yet ceased. If anything, it had become more intense and, now that everyone had woken up, they were taking a little more notice of the downpour.

As people went to bed, the drizzle had already been upgraded through rain and downpour to 'cats and dogs.' As in, it was raining cats and dogs. Not real cats and dogs, of course. That would simply be ridiculous. And dangerous too. If a dog fell out of the sky and hit you on the head, it might give you a very nasty shock not to mention a bump on the noggin! What it means is that when the rain fell on the ground, the puddles were in the shapes of cats and dogs.

Next morning, the people of the village ate their breakfast in silence. Not one of them had ever seen rain like this. It came from the sky in thick sheets, falling out of evil looking black clouds and making huge splashes as the raindrops hit the ground. They ate in silence partly because they couldn't understand this rain that had come from nowhere and partly because the noise of the raindrops falling on the roof was so loud, they couldn't hear one another anyway.

The day dragged on and the rain got heavier. There was even a bit of thunder and lightning which frightened all the babies. One day became two days. Two became three and before anyone knew it, rain had been falling for over two weeks without stopping.

There was one thing about the rain that was the absolute worst: it just made people so miserable. It seemed like overnight there was no more joy (as in happiness – not Joy the person!) in the Village At The End Of The World. There used to be singing and dancing and jokes and laughing. These days, people wanted to just stay at home with a nice hot cup of cocoa and tell sad stories about the good old days. To be fair, there was an up side to all this rain. Grandpa and his monkey police force had nothing to do. Nobody was going to commit a crime with all this rain pouring from the sky.

Sadly, neighbours no longer spoke. Babies didn't have clean nappies. Nobody was drinking enough milk. It was all because of the rain. Nobody wanted to go outside in the torrential rain and risk being soaked to the skin. You couldn't walk next door to borrow some sugar without a full change of clothes when you came back. *And* the sugar would have dissolved in the rain before you made it back to your porch.

Braving the rain, Mr. Hubert Q. Lion called a meeting of his best advisers: Wilson (the deputy mayor), Pete, Baz, the conductor who was in town and Grandpa. All five men and one lion were drenched as they met in the sun room of the Lion residence. Fat lot of good a sun room was when there was all this rain. With all the windows in the sun room, it was even more depressing to watch the rain trickling down the panes of glass.

Something had to be done about this rain. Aside from anything else, it was slowly washing the Village At The End Of The World into the ocean. Chihuahua, who was an incredibly curious young lady, had noticed this while playing in the rain. She had told her father and when Baz told the rest of the group, it gave them the motivation to solve this problem. As they sat drinking hot tea to help them dry off, they went round in a circle to see if anyone had any ideas or experience of what they might do about the pelting rain.

Only Pete was able to offer any kind of an idea of how they might deal with it. What he said went something like this.

"When I was little, my dad told me a story that his uncle told him. Apparently, the uncle's daughter had a kitten that was the son of a cat that was owned by a bus driver back in the Big City. The bus driver had once met Roger, the King of the North who had three sons and a daughter. The middle son was very tall and had won a competition once for being so tall. One of the judges of that competition owned a horse that had been able to talk. During a particularly heavy rain shower, the horse had suggested to a little boy that he should talk to Meredith, the Sunshine Fairy if he wanted the rain to stop."

Of course, the real story that the uncle had told Pete's father was filled with excitement and suspense but that's not what's important. What's crucial is that if the story was true, which it probably wasn't, then someone called Meredith, the Sunshine Fairy might be able to help them. With nothing to lose, Pete was given the task of finding this sunshine fairy and bringing her back to the village to deal with this horrible rainstorm.

That very afternoon, Pete set off to find the fairy. Dressed in galoshes, kagoules and everything necessary to protect you from the rain, he began the journey towards the Big City. Pete's father had cashed in his life insurance many years ago but as far as Pete, knew, the uncle hadn't died yet. He hadn't seen his uncle in a long, long time and hoped he was still alive. Yet when he arrived at the uncle's door, something seemed amiss. His uncle's worn out wellington boots were always on the step but today they were missing. As Pete rang the doorbell, he was greeted by an unfamiliar face. The uncle had put on his wellie boots one day and gone out, never to return.

It was time for Pete to do some detective work. With some excellent sleuthing (actually, he looked it up in the phone book), Pete found the uncle's daughter, his cousin, who was alive and well working as a receptionist in a big, spacious office that was all glass, mahogany and filing cabinets. The kitten had met a sticky end ages ago; something to do with a bottle of whiskey, a power cut and a new frock. For some reason, Pete's cousin didn't want to talk about it too much.

She did manage to find a phone number for the now retired bus driver who owned the poor kitten's mother. It didn't take long for Pete to get him to write a letter of introduction to Roger, the King of the North. After travelling to Roger's castle, he was informed by the guards that Roger had been slain by a dragon just a few days ago. However, his oldest son was now the king. Like sitting in the waiting room at the dentist, Pete had to wait for a long time to see the king who listened for less than one minute and told Pete to stop wasting his time.

Pete was just about to admit defeat when the most enormous horse he had ever seen came parading past him and there, atop the horse, was what looked like a giant to Pete. Finally, some luck in his quest. Pete stopped the horse and asked the prince about the competition. Luckily, the prince was able to remember the names of the three judges in the competition.

On the return to the Big City, Pete (with the help of the phone book again)

found all three judges. The first one laughed at him; the
idea of a talking horse was just ridiculous. The second
one chased him away from his house, thinking him to
be some kind of crazy man. The third judge, however,
was intrigued as to how Pete had found him. It was true:
he did indeed have a horse who could talk and Pete had
arrived not a moment too soon. The horse was sick.
Really sick in fact. It was so sick that the vets didn't
think it would last through the night.

Pete and the judge went immediately to see the
horse who, as it happened was also called Pete, but
that's not important right now. Pete the person began to
talk with Pete the horse about Meredith the Sunshine
Fairy. To begin with, Pete (the horse) was delirious and
Pete (the person) could make no sense of what he was
saying. Yet with his last breath, Pete the horse told Pete
the person where to find Meredith the Sunshine Fairy.
Yet as he heard it, Pete the person's face fell. Pete the
horse had told him something that was exactly what he
didn't want to hear.

Pete the horse had said, "There's a...crossroads just
outside of town...you'll find a...farmer there...who
always loses...his animals...He's the only...one who knows
where...to find...Meredith...the ...Sunshine... F...F...F............."
Pete remembered the last time anyone had seen this
particular farmer. He kept losing his animals because

they were continually on strike since he was such a bad
farmer. He was also an idiot. It was well nigh
impossible to get him to give you any sensible
information.

Yet this was the end of his trail. The horse had died
and gone to heaven. There was nothing else for it but to
go and talk to the farmer. A short walk outside the city
found the same farmer chewing on a piece of straw and
holding court with his pigs who were rolling around in
the dirt. If anything, this simpleton had become more
insane since the last time someone from the Village At
The End Of The World had unfortunately come across
him.

Pete had heard all the stories about this half-wit
and so prepared himself to try to reason with the mad
man. Pete asked very politely, "Pardon me sir, I wonder
if you could tell me where I might find Meredith the
Sunshine Fairy?" As he asked this most simple of
questions, a look of mystery came over the farmer's eyes.
Reaching into the leather satchel that he wore over his
should he produced a glass jar which glowed and
sparkled.

"Take her. I don't want her
any more. She's brought me
nothing but bad news ever since I
caught her. She's the one that makes all my

animals go on strike. Take her and never bring her back.
I don't want to see her again," said the farmer.

Without arguing, Wilson allowed the farmer to
press the jam jar into his hands. With that, the farmer
gathered up his pigs and went on his way. Pete was
taken aback by the unexpected success of his quest. The
farmer was gone before Pete even had time to thank
him. There was nothing else for it. He would begin his
journey back to the Village At The End Of The World
right away. Back to the Big City and onto the empty milk
train, Pete was back in the village before you can say
'Sunshine Fairy Saves The Day.' In all, it had take him
three weeks, two days, sixteen hours, thirty seven
minutes and nine seconds to find Meredith the
Sunshine Fairy and bring her to the village.

As he expected, Pete was *not* met by a welcoming
committee. Everyone was still sheltering from the rain
inside their houses. Pete put his hand into his shoulder
bag to find the jar containing the sunshine fairy where
he found a note that had magically appeared from
nowhere.

My name is Meredith, the Sunshine Fairy. Please help me.
the farmer has imprisoned me inside this jar for ages.
i just want to get out and stretch my wings a bit.
if you set me free, i promise i'll bring you sunshine for
the rest of your days. that's why i'm called the Sunshine Fairy.

Please, please, please let me out.
Meredith, the Sunshine Fairy

So, without a second though, Pete twisted the lid of the jam jar. Then, something he didn't expect happened. There was a beam of light that burst from the jar and went straight up in the air into the evil black clouds that were still pouring gallon after gallon of rain on the Village At The End Of The World. As soon as the light touched the clouds, they too exploded with light. The burst of light spread like a wave all across the sky and then, as if a tap was switched off, the rain stopped.

As the light faded, the villagers looked out their windows and up at the clear blue skies with a yellow sun the colour of sunflowers shone and dried up all the rain. Pete turned around and there behind him, the size of a normal woman, stood Meredith the Sunshine Fairy. She was beautiful. Her shining wings raised high behind her. Without a word, she kissed Pete softly on the cheek and with another burst of light, she shot up in the air.

The story doesn't finish there, however, because after less than five seconds, she landed lightly on the ground where she had stood only moments before. This time, she grabbed Pete around the neck and planted a huge big smacking kiss right on his lips.

But that is another story entirely...

the herald's dais

During one of the weekly brainstorming sessions between Mr. Hubert Q. Lion (the mayor) and Wilson (the deputy mayor), the problem arose of how they might more efficiently spread information in the village. After all, their population had now grown to a size where it was no longer possible to simply go from door to door to tell people the news. What was needed was a method of disseminating information quickly and reliably. Wilson suggested that maybe nothing needed to be done. News travelled through the village quickly along the gossip tree that was well established. However, Mr. Hubert Q. Lion reminded him that this was by no means a reliable method of distributing information.

Wilson remained unconvinced that they needed to take action, so Mr. Hubert Q. Lion decided to conduct an experiment to convince Wilson of what he meant. As two cello players were passing his office window, he casually mentioned that his paws had been giving him a little bother recently. He said it just loud enough for the cello players to hear him. Wilson didn't think any more about it until later that afternoon when Chihuahua appeared at the door to their office with a basket of fruit and a bottle with a very strange label:

Dr. Ebenezer Finkelbottom's Ointment For Lame Lions

"I heard you can't walk any more so I've brought you some fruit because that's what you give to sick people because it's good for them and has lots of vitamins. Oh, and I brought this ointment that my dad said would make you better," said Chihuahua.

Mr. Hubert Q. Lion looked knowingly at Wilson and said, "Oh, thank you Chihuahua. Why don't you leave the ointment here and I'll put it on my feet before I go to bed. And thank you so much for the fruit. You're really a special girl you know. But how did you know I was lame?"

"Well," said Chihuahua, "some cello players overheard you talking in your office and they happened to mention it to Joy. Joy was buying her milk at the same time as Pete who told one of the flute players

who met Grandpa and Lonely Jake in the village green.
Lonely Jake had lunch with Bob who had some
business with the King of the Ants. The ants were
helping the men who play the big drums with
something who told my mum who told my dad who
told my grandmother who told Bob who told me. So
here I am."

When she finally finished and left, Mr. Hubert Q.
Lion poured the ointment down the sink. "Humph! Dr.
Ebenezer Finkelbottom's Ointment For Lame Lions
indeed! Reluctantly, Wilson had to admit that maybe
gossip wasn't the most reliable way of spreading news in
the village – it was just like a huge game of Chinese
whispers.

It was then that Wilson remembered something he
had seen in one of the other villages he had been to
while looking for Mr. Hubert Q. Lion. That village had a
town herald and a little platform in the middle of the
village green called a dais. Any time they wanted to tell
the people of the village some important piece of news
or some vital information for their survival, the herald
would climb on his platform and announce
it at the top of his voice. Maybe that might
work in the Village At The End Of The
World.

Mr. Hubert Q. Lion seized on the idea

immediately and set about preparing a sign for the auditions...

POSITION VACANT:
Village At THe end of THe world HerAld

Duties to include:
THe ANNouNcement of imPortANt News AND iNformAtioN from the dAis (to be coNStructed) oN the villAge green.

Previous quAlificAtioNs/exPerieNce:
NoNe NecessArY

PAY:
ONe PouNd, 4 SHilliNgS AND SixPeNce Per week Plus All the APPles You cAN eAt

APPlicAtioN DeAdliNe:
Tomorrow At NooN.
Collect APPlicAtioNs forms from the MAYor's office.

** WomeN Need Not APPlY: Too ProNe To GoSSiPiNg **

That very afternoon, Mr. Hubert Q. Lion tacked his notice to the noticeboard outside the village hall so that everyone could see it. He had even thought to write his notice on bright pink paper so that it would be more eye-catching. Such a controversial notice caused an uproar in the village. One half of the village (the men) were excited at the opportunity for a new job, especially one that paid so well. The other half of the village (the women) were furious that women were not allowed to apply for the job. As if to prove Mr. Hubert Q. Lion's point, the women spent most of the rest of that day gossiping about the whole proceeding. 'Isn't it shocking how they won't let women apply for the job!' 'I wouldn't want the job anyway!' 'I'm sure my Mick will get the job: he has the loudest voice in the village!'

There was a flurry of activity the next morning as Mr. Hubert Q. Lion and Wilson arrived at work. A long line (possibly too long) of men waited outside their office, ready to pick up the forms. Mr. Hubert Q. Lion began handing out the forms one by one while Wilson went to find Grandpa who soon appeared with his police force and started hauling all the women out of the line who were dressed up as men. It was their high pitched voices that gave them away.

By noon, forty seven men from the Village At The End Of The World had completed the application forms and were waiting in a long line outside the mayor's office once again. This time they were waiting for a chance to see how loud their voice was.

Wilson had devised a points system and the men were marked on volume, intelligibility (which is a fancy way of saying whether or not you could understand what they were shouting) and timbre (which is a fancy way of saying if it was a nice voice to listen to or not). The mayor and deputy mayor heard all kinds of voices that afternoon from deep growls that made the ground rumbles to high pitched squeals that sounded distinctly like a girl. In fact, the more Wilson thought about it, the more certain he was that it really was a girl. Grandpa was once again called and Chihuahua was dragged out of the room kicking and screaming, furious that she had been caught.

By dinnertime, the original field of forty seven had been narrowed to a short list of five candidates who were informed that they should return the next morning for a second round of auditions. They all had excellent qualifications: an opera singer, an auctioneer, a sheep dog trainer, a football commentator and a preacher. All of them were well known professions for people with loud, strong voices.

Next morning, a strange sickness had descended on the Village At The End Of The World. What made it so strange was that it only seemed to affect the men of the village. The women were up early taking care of their chores as usual but every man in the village remained in bed. Their wives pretended to be concerned for their husbands, brothers and sons. They did all the things that you should do for someone who is sick. They felt their foreheads for a temperature. They poked and prodded a little bit and then they asked them to say 'Aaahhh' and looked inside their mouths. When they did, they saw ugly purple and green spots at the back of the men's mouths. The worst part of it was that they had all lost their voices. Not a single man in the village could speak even one word. All they could do was try to communicate in a hoarse whisper. To double the confusion, both Mr. Hubert Q. Lion and Wilson were also confined to their beds with the same affliction.

What the husbands didn't know was that their wives had carefully mixed in a very special fruit with their dinner. It wasn't anything serious: it just made you lose your voice for 24 hours. They were so angry at Mr. Hubert Q. Lion's discrimination against women, they decided to take matters into their own hands. It had all been Princess Lydia's idea.

Once the men had all been told to remain in bed for a couple of days by their wives, all the women of the village met together on the village green. Princess Lydia stood on a rickety platform that had been hastily constructed from some old orange crates. She began by letting out a huge roar that attracted the attention not only of all the assembled women but also every man who was lying in his bed. Now that everyone was listening, she explained her plan. They would restart the application process, except this time only women would be allowed to apply. There would be no forms to fill in. All the women would have to do would be to shout at the top of their voices. Princess Lydia and Joy would be the judges since neither one of them had any desire to be the town herald.

As the day wore on, the candidates just seemed to get louder and louder. Unfortunately, the louder they became, the less you could understand them. They had prepared a short speech for each woman to shout which went like this:

"People of the Village At The End Of The World, hear ye, hear ye, hear ye. It is with great pleasure that I, [insert name here] am the new herald of our fair village. I will serve you diligently to the best of my ability, always passing on the news quickly and without bias. I thank you."

The best candidates were mostly understood by the judges. The worst ones sounded a bit like this:

"People of the Villaaaaaaa Aaa Nnnnçççç Ffffffff Waaaaaaad..." and so it continued.

The men of the village were lying in their sick beds for all this time with nothing else to do but listen to everything that was going on. To begin with, it was a source of great amusement to them but as the day went on and they began to realise how serious the women were, they really started to get worried. Some of the women that they had listened to had been simply awful. On Wilson's marking scheme, they would have been awarded ten marks for loudness and zero for intelligibility and timbre.

Just as with the men's auditions, Princess Lydia and Joy came up with a short list of just five women who they thought had what it takes to be the village herald. The women weren't foolish enough to leave the final decision until the next day. They knew they had to make their decision that very night.

They decided to have a little bit of a break and to go home to check on their husbands to make sure they were still OK. After all, they still loved them and wanted to make sure that they weren't too sick. Yet despite the men's best efforts to get the women to talk about what was going on, Princess Lydia had made them all take a vow of secrecy that they wouldn't tell the men who any of the short listed candidates were.

After the village had eaten its dinner, the women once again collected at the village green. There was a carnival atmosphere in the air. Someone had brought some leftover apple pie. Fairy lanterns were strung between the lamp posts and somehow, someone had found the time to construct a proper herald's dais. It was an artistic masterpiece of beautiful carved and twisted wood that any herald would be proud to stand atop and announce the news.

The judging panel had been expanded to include Chihuahua, her mother and her grandmother who, it was hoped, could bring some extra insight and wisdom into the final decision. Without any further ado, the five remaining applicants began roaring with all their might. To be honest, they were all very good but there was just something missing. The judges listened to them one by one, all together, in groups and every which way they could think of. With each passing minute, the five judges began to lose hope. All five of these ladies were fairly good. They just weren't of the calibre that they felt was needed for a village herald. Although the five women tried their hardest, they just didn't impress the judges enough for anyone of them to be declared the outright winner.

This was certainly a big problem indeed. The women had made all of their husbands sick so that one of them could be the herald and now, the five best candidates simply weren't good enough. The entire judging panel retired to the mayor's office. It was empty, since Mr. Hubert Q. Lion and Wilson were still in their sick beds. They also took the five finalists with them to see if any of them could shed any light on what was to be done.

Long into the night, the ten women talked about what might be a solution to their problem. All kinds of ideas were suggested and then discounted. The silence from the village green was unnerving. The rest of the women had gone home to their husbands and nobody was screaming or shouting any more.

Finally, just before midnight, Princess Lydia once again climbed onto the herald's dais and with an opening roar, she made her announcement. "Men and women of the Village At The End Of The World, hear ye, hear ye, hear ye. Thank you for your patience. The judging panel has decided on the new herald for our village. That person's name will be announced at 9:18am precisely tomorrow morning. Thank you and good night."

Next morning, the men of the village were back to full health and the whole village turned out for the announcement to find out who the herald for the village would be. When the population of the Village At The End Of The World arrived at the herald's dais, they were taken aback at the intricacy of the designs and carvings on the dais. They had never seen something so beautiful before. Somebody had put an awful lot of work into making this dais. Another thing that surprised the people were the red velvet ropes that had been erected in a circle all around the dais.

By a quarter past nine, the whole village was there waiting for the new herald to make themselves known. Finally, at 9:18am precisely, Princess Lydia climbed the dais once again and with her now customary roar, she made her annunciation. "People of the Village At The End Of The World, hear ye, hear ye, hear ye. It is with great pleasure that I, Princess Lydia Lion, am the new herald of our fair village. I will serve you diligently to the best of my ability, always passing on the news quickly and without bias. I thank you."

All the women of the village began cheering while the men simply stood and stared with mouths aghast. How had they been tricked like this? Somehow a woman had become the herald of the Village At The End Of The World. No-one was more surprised than Mr.

Hubert Q. Lion who suddenly realised that his own wife had plotted behind his back.

When Princess Lydia finished her speech, she hung a sign on the front of the dais, walked down the steps and into the cheering crowd.

pere jacques and padre diego

One lazy Thursday lunch time, the mayor and the
deputy mayor had more or less finished their business
for the day and were settling down for their customary
afternoon nap. Wilson had finished his apple, thrown
the core into the bin (ever since the plague of ants, he
always used a bin), propped his size eleven feet on the
corner of the desk and was in the process of slowly
nodding off. Mr. Hubert Q. Lion had finished grooming
himself and was settling down to sleep on a special
giant pillow that Chihuahua's grandmother had made
especially.

What they both failed to notice, as did most of the
rest of the village, was the two men who arrived in the
village along the Village At The End Of The World
Highway. This was not remarkable in itself:
occasionally visitors would arrive in the village. What
was odd about these two men was that they were dressed
almost identically yet they were very clearly not
travelling together. In fact, they were making every
effort to stay as far away from one another as possible

which isn't easy to do an a narrow road.

Each man wore an uncomfortable brown tunic that was tied at the waist with some coarse string. Around their necks, they each wore a funny white collar. Each man had a donkey and a cart which seemed to be loaded with their entire worldly possessions: worn and battered pots and pans, a dusty mattress and a few tattered old books. The donkeys were both old and the men had to cajole them every inch of the way.

This strange procession stopped for a long time outside the church that had been built especially for the recent weddings of Bob & Joy and Mr. Hubert Q. and Princess Lydia Lion. Both men looked suspiciously at the church, then at one another and then back at the church again. There was definitely something very odd going on here.

Both men presented themselves at the village hall at the same moment, just as Hubert and Wilson were slipping off into their afternoon dreamland. That was when the argument began. Each man demanded that he be heard first by the mayor. Eventually, the only way to settle the dispute was for the mayor to see one man and the deputy mayor to see the other. Then, they would swap over.

Père Jacques was the first to see Mr. Hubert Q. Lion. He explained with a thick French accent that his order, the Brotherhood of Perpetual Ferocity had heard of a church in the Village At The End Of The World that needed someone to take care of it. As a result, he was here as their new priest. He would build himself a house and take over as priest-in-charge of the Village At The End Of The World Chapel without further delay.

This all seemed like a good idea to Mr. Hubert Q. Lion and so he consented to Père Jacques' wishes and even offered help in any way it was needed. Père Jacques could begin building his house right away. As he departed, Père Jacques was all smiles, shaking paws with the mayor and deputy mayor.

Next, Padre Diego was shown into the mayor's parlour. He explained with a thick Spanish accent that his order, the Brotherhood of Everlasting Hostility had heard of a church in the Village At The End Of The World that needed someone to take care of it. As a result, he was here as their new priest. He would build himself a house and take over as priest-in-charge of the Village At The End Of The World Chapel without further delay.

Despite a certain amount of déjà vu, Mr. Hubert Q. Lion consented to Padre Diego's wishes. After all, two

priests were better than one. Weren't they? Mr. Hubert
Q. Lion and Wilson settled back down at their
respective desks. As they were idling the afternoon away
napping, Wilson drifted in and out of sleep. Something
worried him: the names of the orders. What was it they
had been called. After an hour of fitful dreaming,
Wilson suddenly sat bolt upright. The Brotherhood of
Perpetual Ferocity? The Brotherhood of Everlasting
Hostility? Surely that wasn't a good thing? If only he
had known quite the trouble it would cause, he would
have expelled both priests from the village there
and then. However, Mr. Hubert Q. Lion assured him
that his fears were unfounded and Wilson soon fell
back asleep, succumbing to the heat of the
afternoon.

To get anywhere in the Village At The End Of
The World, one almost always had to
walk through the big green in the
middle of the village. So it was that as
Wilson and Mr. Hubert Q. Lion strolled
home together in the evening, they watched the
sun setting behind the church spire on the
west side of the green. The still and quiet of
the sunset was disturbed by the sounds of
construction. On the north side of the green,
someone was sawing wood as if their life

depended on it. On the south side of the green, someone else was hammering as if tomorrow wasn't going to come. Looking to their left and right, they saw the signs:

> PÈRE JACQUES
>
> BROTHERHOOD OF PERPETUAL FEROCITY

> PADRE DIEGO
>
> BROTHERHOOD OF EVERLASTING HOSTILITY

A sense of foreboding came over both Wilson and Mr. Hubert Q. Lion. From the style of construction, they could tell that something was very far amiss here. They couldn't quite put their finger on it but clearly neither of these houses was designed to be a normal house. Despite their best attempts, neither Père Jacques or Padre Diego was willing to stop their work even for a minute to discuss what was going on.

Walking to work the next morning, Mr. Hubert Q. Lion and Wilson could see exactly what was going on: these houses were being built for defence. Both of the priests had been working all night. Père Jacques had spent the night working on the walls and roof of his house which were complete with battlements on the top. The barrel of a cannon could be seen poking through a gun turret on the roof. Padre Diego, on the

other hand, had spent the night improving the external
defences. A deep moat had been dug all the way around
the foundations and the padre was currently filling it
with buckets of sea water that he carried, one in each
hand.

Within a week, Père Jacques and Padre Diego had
both finished their houses. Their signs had been altered
slightly too:

These two monstrosities were a mixture of the old
and new: battlements, portcullises and drawbridges
alongside razor wire, security cameras and high-tech
weapons systems. It was clear that neither of these
priests had come to look after the church, at least not to
begin with. First, they had to fight it out to the death.

The Village At The End Of The World was gripped
with the melodrama of it all. An enterprising pair of

trombone players erected bleachers on the east side of the village green and sold tickets: two for a shilling. People could come and watch this epic battle that was about to take place in their village. The Violinist's Dairy Co-Operative changed the label on their milk in honour of the occasion. Everyone chose sides for who they wanted to win the battle. However, this was usually a somewhat arbitrary decision. It often went along the lines of, 'I much prefer French food so I want Père Jacques to win the battle,' or, 'My grandma got a postcard from Spain once so I want Padre Diego to win.'

The tickets for the grandstand sold like hot cakes and before long they were sold out. Oddly enough, nobody was particularly worried about being hit by a stray bullet or a poorly aimed arrow. Yet since neither Père Jacques nor Padre Diego had shared with anyone when they planned to start fighting, the trombone players erected a siren on top of the church steeple. They spread the word that when the siren went off, that was the sign that the battle was about to start.

Only Chihuahua's father, Baz, was particularly worried about what might happen with this 'war fever' that had swept their village. Sitting in the mayor's office, he explained to Mr. Hubert Q. Lion and Wilson that when he was a little boy, his grandmother had told him a story. He couldn't remember much about that story but he did remember that it had been about the Brothers of Perpetual Ferocity and the Brothers of Everlasting Hostility. They had been enemies since before anyone could remember and their battles were well known for their 'collateral damage' which is a nice way of saying that lots of people get killed whether they are involved or not. They simply had to stop this battle or else a whole lot of people were going to die, whether they liked it or not.

As Baz finished explaining their predicament, he heard the sound that he dreaded: the piercing wail of the siren at the top of the church spire. Instead of running away and hiding (which is the normal response to a siren), the entire village dropped what they were doing and ran *towards* the sound. Mr. Hubert Q. Lion, Wilson and Baz burst onto the village green just in time to see the two trombone players collecting tickets and selling hot dogs. With music playing, the atmosphere was just like a football game.

The security cameras on front of the Castle Of The Brotherhood Of Perpetual Ferocity twisted and turned, having a good look at the bleachers, the church and the Fortress Of The Brotherhood Of Everlasting Hostility. The cameras on the front of the other 'house' did exactly the same. Suddenly, as if on a signal, the cameras stopped moving. Each one was trained on the opposite 'house.' A deadly hush descended on the crowd. Some sat with a hot dog half way to their mouth. Others were in mid conversation and just stayed there with their mouths open. Every person knew that this was it.

Suddenly, without warning, all hell broke loose. The high-tech weapons systems began their opening barrages. Missiles, tracer bullets, mortars, flares and the contents of a huge military arsenal were unleashed across the peaceful village green in the first minutes of the war. A stray mortar landed a little bit too close for comfort to the audience, right on top of the hot dog machine. As the sausages rained down on the crowd, there was pandemonium. Everyone was panicking, trying to escape the village green. The trombone players were in uproar, demanding to know who was going to pay for all of the hot dogs that had been destroyed.

Just as the last cello player had escaped from the crossfire, the heavy artillery stopped as quickly as it had begun. Père Jacques and Padre Diego had both run out of ammunition simultaneously and were now preparing to fight this battle 'old school.' A frantic hammering came from both sides of the green. In less than an hour, both priests had completed construction of their trebuchets, a type of catapult. Without even a break to catch their breath, all manner of things began flying across the village green, launched with force from the trebuchets: rocks, bits of wood, rotten vegetables, rotten fish and at one point a live cow.

By now, the crowd had returned. After all, the priests' aim was exceptional with the trebuchets so they felt safe on the bleachers, out of the way of the battle. However, another panic ensued when, as the cow was ejected from the trebuchet, a rope broke changing the aim of the airborne bovine. As it passed over the heads of the audience, it did what cows do best and pooped right on the heads of the watching crowd.

As the priests attempted to fire heavier and heavier objects at one another, this took its toll on the hastily constructed trebuchets. It wasn't long before these most ancient weapons of war were reduced to kindling.

Without a pause, Père Jacques and Padre Diego mounted the battlements of their respective fortresses. They began raining arrows from their heavy longbows on one another. Many of these arrows overshot or undershot their marks, coming dangerously close to the ever expanding crowds. Yet just as with the other attempts, the priests soon ran out of arrows and were forced into a situation that neither wanted: close combat.

With the cranking of chains and metal scraping against metal, the portcullises were raised. With an enormous thump, the drawbridges dropped and there at the entrance to each castle were the two warriors. Each man was perched atop his stubborn mule (who was idly chewing on the buttercups growing around the castle). They were no longer dressed in their simple brown cassocks. Now they wore full armour including helmet and feather plume. Père Jacques' feathers were red and Padre Diego had blue quills in his helmet. As one, they geed their donkeys who refused to move, more interested in the buttercups.

Père Jacques and Padre Diego dismounted from their disloyal steeds and each let out a bloodcurdling war cry. With swords held aloft, they ran towards one another, ready to finish this and fight to the death. Before their swords crossed for the first time, however, a third knight burst through the doors of the church, out into the sunlight. This night was dressed in shining silver armour with a white plume from his helmet. Neither priest fully understood what was happening but paused just long enough to hear the terrifying scream that emanated from inside the white knight's helmet, 'THIS CHURCH HAS A PRIEST ALREADY!

AAAAAAAARRRRGGGHHH!!!!'

Père Jacques and Padre Diego looked at one another and then back at the white knight. He was running across the green towards them with not one but two swords slicing through the air. Closer and closer he came and in that moment, the two priests made a decision: The Village At The End Of The World could have their priest. This white knight was about to kill them both. So they turned on their tails and ran as fast as their legs would carry them and as fast as their armour would let them. They ran past the bleachers on the east side of the square, through the village and on towards the Village At The End Of The World Highway. That was the last anyone ever heard of Père Jacques and Padre Diego.

The crowd turned its attention back to the village green, to the white knight who had mysteriously appeared from the church. The anticipation was tortuous as Mr. Hubert Q. Lion approached the white knight to find out who he was. Painfully slowly, the knight removed his helmet and there, glistening with sweat, was Baz.

'I've had this old suit of armour lying around the house for ages. Found it at the side of the road once. I kept it just in case I ever needed it. It's lucky I never threw it out, eh? Chihuahua used to play dress up with it but it's nice to use it for the real thing again.'

dr. baz's hair restoral ointment

Much has been written about the arrival of the
various residents in the Village At The End Of The
World: Mr. Hubert Q. Lion, Wilson, Bob and Joy
(accompanied by their respective symphony
orchestras), Pete, the five monkeys (Grandpa, Big Rab,
Lonely Jake, Fred and The Leaf) and of course Princess
Lydia and her butterflies. However, we never did find
out how the original five residents made it to the village.
It had, up until now remained a mystery to everyone
who lived in the village. Of course, it was a matter of
great speculation, particularly amongst the violinists
who were well known for their tall tales. Something of
such little import but such immense mystery was
perfect fodder for their bedtime stories and
afternoon tales.

Chihuahua and her family
remained silent on the subject, no matter
how much they were pressed for the truth.
It was, they informed their interrogators, a

family matter that concerned no-one else but blood relatives. For a long time, this answer satisfied everyone who wanted to know the truth or at least, if not satisfied, they were deterred from digging any deeper.

That was until one misty morning when something came along the Village At The End Of The World Highway that changed everyone's minds about Chihuahua and her family. Into the village green rolled a horse and cart. Yet this was no normal horse. It was a like a giant with a plaited mane and flowers woven into its tail. It wore a straw hat over its bleached blonde ears which contrasted with the chocolate brown of the rest of its body. The cart was as odd as the horse. It had been yellow at one stage of its life but the worn and battered yellow paint was now covered with a whole host of painted flowers and a sign painted in old style writing:

Dr. Ebenezer Finkelbottom's
Travelling Surgery

Doctor, Dentist, Optician, Pharmacist, Chiropodist, Psychiatrist, Veterinarian

The importance of this new arrival was treated with great interest and word soon spread of this medical professional who had arrived in the village. *Everyone* had a complaint that they wanted to talk to Dr. Finkelbottom about. Only seven people in the village had any idea that this may not be the blessing that it first appeared to be: the five original residents of the village, Mr. Hubert Q. Lion and Wilson.

Dr. Ebenezer Finkelbottom was stranger than his horse and cart put together. A wiry old man with a bald head and a beard and moustache to be proud of, he climbed down from the driver's seat and dusted himself down from travelling. On his head he wore a battered old top hat that gave him an air of faded glory. A green and yellow striped waistcoat and a purple bowtie were worn over a shirt that had once been blue but had been repaired many times with a wide variety of fabrics and colours. His grey slacks were likewise oft mended and his toes poked through the holes in his socks and right through the holes in his shoes too.

Without wasting a moment, Finkelbottom opened the wooden shutters on the side of his cart to reveal an astonishing collection of potions and lotions. Once he had carefully tied the shutters back, he removed two folding wooden chairs and a complicated fabric screen with a metal frame. After wrestling with the chair and screen for a few minutes, he had finally finished setting up his consultation room. With a final flourish, set out another sign.

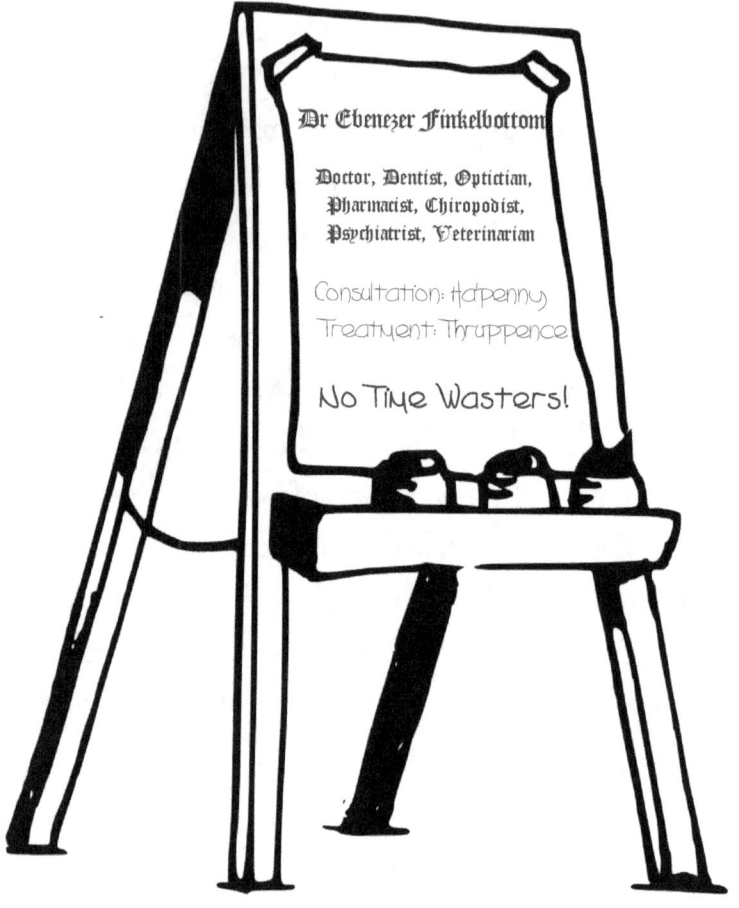

With no discussion or fuss, a line of people formed starting at the sign and twisting unevenly around the village green. The line was full of people with corns and bunions, or a funny rash on their tummy, or a toothache (or seven or eight), or a sick puppy (one sick rhinoceros but that is another story entirely), or one leg shorter than the other.

Mr. Hubert Q. Lion and Wilson watched from the edge of the green with a mixture of bemusement and disbelief. They weren't quite sure what to make of the doctor and his travelling surgery. Something worried Wilson; he had heard that name somewhere before. It was on the tip of his tongue but before he could remember it, Baz happened by the mayor and the deputy mayor with a very worried look on his face. "We need to talk," he said without emotion. In the mayor's office, Baz sat down to tell his story.

"A long time ago now, my family and I lived in the Big City. There was me, my wife Victoria and my mother, Maria. My wife was going to have a baby too. We were so happy, we thought life couldn't get any better."

"My mother is an old gypsy woman and she often knows things that other people do not. So when she came to me one day and told me about a business opportunity that I simply had to invest in, I knew that she was onto a winner."

"I bought a franchise of Dr. Ebenezer Finkelbottom's Travelling Surgery. It was a surefire success at business. They set you up with your own horse and cart, provide you with all of their potions and even print up phoney medical certificates to make you look like you're legitimate. Oh, they give you a bit of training – show you how to pull a tooth out and that kind of thing but really it's all a big scam."

"Anyway, the business model involves travelling to far away villages where the simpleton villagers don't know any better and peddling the fake potions. Of course, by the time the residents of a village realised they had been conned, you would be long gone."

"With a young family and the advice of my gypsy mother, I invested everything I had in getting a piece of the pie. I became one of just twenty Dr. Ebenezer Finkelbottoms who were peddling their fake wares around the country."

"For a few weeks, life was good and the money was rolling in. Just like his sign says, consultation was a ha'penny and treatment was thruppence. The big money was in the treatment which was in most cases water with a little bit of food colouring added to make it look expensive."

"There were one or two cures that we had that actually worked, however. In fact, if a village was reluctant to spend their money on our 'cures,' we would find a few volunteers to cure for free. Of course, we couldn't magically cure someone's broken leg or anything like that – that only happens in the movies. We did have a good cure for bunions though. The

problem was that about a week after the bunions were
cured, some rather odd blue spots would appear on the
soles of the feet that would never go away. Ever. So we
had to make sure that we'd moved on before the week
was out, no matter how good business was. We also had
a really remarkable cure for lame lions. No side effects
and one hundred percent effective. In fact, that's the
stuff I sent over a couple of weeks ago to cure your
lameness. It obviously worked like a charm for you."

Mr. Hubert Q. Lion didn't have the heart to tell Baz
that he had actually poured the potion down the plug
hole so he simply grunted, "Hmm, yes," and let Baz
continue.

"Just before our baby was due to be born, my
mother suggested I went to one more village to earn
some money. Then I should take a holiday to help
Victoria with the baby. So I plaited my horse's hair and
set off for a village that I knew no Dr. Ebenezer
Finkelbottom had ever visited. What I didn't know was
that one of the other franchisees had visited the
next village over just two weeks before.
Those people were furious about the blue
spots on their feet and word had spread
that Dr. Ebenezer Finkelbottom's Bunion

Cure was to blame."

"Of course, the general population aren't made aware of the fact that we're a franchise so it wasn't actually me who had been in that village. So when I pulled into this new village with my horse and cart, there was a very definite air of hostility. I thought, 'I've dealt with tough crowds before. I can handle this.' In my attempts to whip the crowd into a frenzy of medical consultation and treatment, I offered to cure a few bunions for free. One old lady in the crowd volunteered without the usual cajoling and persuasion but once she took her old boots off and revealed the ugly blue spots on the soles of her feet, I knew I was in trouble."

"There had to have been at least a hundred people in the crowd. I managed to make it back on to the driver's seat of my cart and geed the horses back on to the highway and away from certain death. Unfortunately, I didn't have time to close the shutters on the cart and my potions left a trail across half the countryside. The people from the village gathered everything up and took it to the police who told them that the only proper cures were the bunion ointment and the cure for lame lions. Everything else was just coloured water. However, since Dr. Ebenezer Finkelbottom hadn't actually done anything that was against the law, they couldn't do anything about it."

"The people of the village decided they could do something about it. They next morning the newspapers hit the streets with my picture on the front page:"

"All over the country, people were up in arms about Dr. Ebenezer Finkelbottom. They were furious that they had been duped. However, there was nobody angrier than the nineteen other Dr. Ebenezer Finkelbottoms who were now baying for my blood. That's why, just before my wife gave birth to Chihuahua, we ran away. We just ran and ran and ran and eventually we came to the Village At The End Of The World. We were (and still are) on the run from Dr. Ebenezer Finkelbottom."

"On the way here, we found the suit of

armour that I was wearing when I scared away Père
Jacques and Padre Diego. It was just lying by the side of
the road but that's not important now. Chihuahua was
born while we were travelling. As a matter of fact, we
had just arrived here when Mr. Hubert Q. Lion showed
up and rescued Chihuahua from the ocean. She was a
strong baby, to be sure!"

Once again, Mr. Hubert Q. Lion didn't have the
heart to tell Baz that he had actually been trying to eat
Chihuahua at the time so again, he grunted, "Hmm,
yes," and let Baz continue.

Except Baz had finished – his story was done. Now
they knew the truth about Dr. Ebenezer Finkelbottom,
they had to decide what could be done about this
swindler who was in their midst. It was clear that the
population of the village trusted his medical skills, even
though Baz, Wilson and Mr. Hubert Q. Lion knew him to
be a fake. Baz had an idea.

Many of the people who Baz had consulted during
his months as Dr. Ebenezer Finkelbottom had been bald
men looking for a more permanent cure than a wig. It
seemed everyone wanted to buy some of Dr. Ebenezer
Finkelbottom's Hair Restoral Cream. In fact, at
thruppence a bottle, it was one of his best sellers. Of
course, it was just water with a bit of green colouring

but it had set Baz thinking. When the franchise had folded and Baz had moved his family to the Village At The End Of The World, he had been secretly working on his own Dr. Baz's Hair Restoral Ointment. After years of work, he had only just perfected it.

Mr. Hubert Q. Lion, Wilson and Baz approached Dr. Ebenezer Finkelbottom with a new business proposal for him. Their suggestion was that he become the sole distributor or Dr. Baz's Hair Restoral Ointment. He would be able to collect fifty percent of the profits. This was like music to Finkelbottom's ears – tired of peddling fake cures, he would finally be able to sell a potion that did exactly what it said on the label. Baz explained that the ointment took one full week to be effective but the doctor didn't mind waiting. It didn't occur to him how much danger he would be in.

The baldest man in the village was fetched, an oboe player who resembled a billiard ball, his head was so shiny. Baz explained that the ointment would be applied once every twenty four hours and at the end of one week, this oboist would have a full head of hair that Rapunzel herself would be jealous of.

Dr. Finkelbottom was somewhat sceptical but, unwilling to pass up such an excellent opportunity, he decided to stick around and wait. He was even more encouraged when, by the end of the first day, a light fuzz had begun to grow on the oboe player's scalp. Nobody was more surprised than the oboe player himself – he had lost all his hair, going bald at the age of sixteen. His head had been cold ever since.

As the days wore on, the man's hair grew longer and longer. By the end of four days, it was quite astonishing. This man had been completely bald just ninety six hours ago and now he had silky brown hair covering his head. Baz and Dr. Finkelbottom sat down to hammer out the details of their agreement. Dr. Finkelbottom would return once a year to pick up more supplies and to drop off the profits. In return, he could fix his own price and even use some of the other Dr. Finkelbottoms to help him distribute this miracle product.

On the seventh day, Baz and Dr. Finkelbottom conducted a careful inspection of the oboists head. Dr. Finkelbottom wanted to make sure that he hadn't been tricked by a wig. Baz wanted to be sure that Dr. Finkelbottom was convinced. With one final application of the ointment, the treatment was complete. Baz shook hands with the doctor and then removed his gloves.

Yet as Dr. Ebenezer Finkelbottom was preparing his cart to leave and waiting for his first consignment of

Dr. Baz's Hair Restoral Ointment, he became aware of a group of villagers standing behind him. As he turned to look at them, he immediately realised his mistake. At least thirty people stood there with bare feet covered with ugly looking blue spots. He had stayed in the village too long and the people had found him out. As he jumped back onto his cart and hurried out of the village, he forgot all about Baz and his hair restoral cream. All he wanted to do was escape from the enraged villagers who wanted to know what he was going to do about the blue spots on their feet.

As a final insult, Dr. Finkelbottom looked at the palm of his right hand where he saw a few faint hairs beginning to sprout. It was then that he remembered that Baz had shaken his hand before removing his gloves. For the rest of his life, Dr. Ebenezer Finkelbottom had the most beautiful brown hair growing from the palm of his right hand where Baz had tricked him and applied the ointment.

the first annual world princess wrestling championships

Ever one to improve the village and boost tourism with interesting cultural events, Mr. Hubert Q. Lion had decided that the time was ripe for a second festival in the year. Of course, the Greatest Concert In The World was a big draw since it was the only place that a concert goer could hear two symphony orchestras performing on the same stage. However, that was just once a year and Mr. Hubert Q. Lion felt that the Village At The End Of The World should think about staging another event to attract the masses. This time, however, he wanted to be a little more alternative in his approach.

The crowd who came on the railway for the Greatest Concert In The World were all very nice but it was just so genteel. They came with their picnics: cucumber   sandwiches, chilled white wine and cheese and crackers. Dressed in their finery, they were quite a spectacle but Mr. Hubert Q. Lion longed for something a little different. He wanted to attract an entirely different section of humanity, to provide something for the humble working classes. The Greatest Concert In The World with its overtures, concertos and sinfoniettas was much too high brow for the people that Mr. Hubert Q. Lion hoped to attract to add some life to the otherwise humdrum life in the Village At The End Of The World.

That is why, on a bitterly cold November morning, Baz and Bob boarded a train bound for the Big City with the following press release:

PRESS RELEASE

From the same people who brought you

The Greatest Concert In The World
and
Père Jacques & Padre Diego: The Final Showdown

comes
**The First Annual
World Princess Wrestling Championships**

All Princesses and Female Nobility Welcome
(Baroness, Earless, Lady, Queen, Marquess, etc.)
Ladies-In-Waiting Accepted As Proxy Wrestlers

First Prize: **A Big Sack Of Money**
Second Prize: **A Small Sack Of Money**
Everyone Else: **BFH** *(Bus Fare Home)*

Come One, Come All
First Round Begins On 1st February at 7:04pm
Final Will Be Fought Come Hell Or High Water On
     1st March at 6:47pm

Baz and Bob had a simple mission: to spread the word about the World Princess Wrestling Championships as far and wide as possible. As they rode on an empty carriage in the milk train, Baz and Bob discussed how they might best spread the news to firstly get a bunch of princesses and other nobility to enter and secondly how to get a whole lot more people to come and watch the wrestling. They decided that the best way was to use radio and newspapers. After all, *everyone* listened to the radio and if they could get on the front page of a newspaper, they'd be sure to be seen.

Somehow, the two managed to get themselves on one of the most popular radio shows in the world on the very first day they were in the Big City. The DJ loved the idea of watching princesses wrestling and, so it seemed, his listeners did too. As soon as they had announced the First Annual World Princess Wrestling Championships, the phones in the radio station's offices began to ring off the hooks. Everyone wanted to know how to enter, how to get tickets and who were these two geniuses who had come up with the idea.

Overnight,   Baz and Bob

became virtual superstars in the Big City. They didn't need to keep publicizing the wrestling: the idea captured the imagination of the whole city. Every newspaper, radio station and television show wanted to have Baz and Bob on to discuss the idea of princesses wrestling. Of course, there were a few critics who were confident that the idea would never catch on but the numbers spoke for themselves: Baz and Bob had already written down the names of 42 princesses, 16 ladies and one baroness who all wanted to participate in the championship. Obviously, the first prize of a big sack of money was quite tempting to all these ladies of nobility.

What Baz and Bob didn't realize was that the prize money had nothing to do with why they had so many competitors signed up. You see, princesses had been wrestling by themselves for many years but always in secret: in special underground wrestling clubs that were only talked about in whispers. When Baz and Bob had gone on the radio, it was a perfect opportunity to bring princess wrestling into the mainstream with someone else footing the bill.

By the end of just one week, Baz and Bob had done a rather sterling job. They had no less than one hundred and thirteen competitors, had sold more than three thousand tickets at sixpence each, had negotiated

with the Big City Railroad Corporation to lay on the
necessary extra trains and had even found some time to
buy some gifts for their wives and loved ones back in
the Village At The End Of The World. Boarding the
empty milk train, they once again set off through the
Giant's Desert, passed through the Land Of The
Windmills and carried on up the Village At The End Of
The World Highway until they were finally home again.

The months of November, December and January
passed frighteningly quickly as the Village At The End
Of The World prepared to host this major sporting
event. Seventeen separate wrestling rings were built
around the village, along with all the seats, hot dog
stands and souvenir stalls that were needed. By mid
January, princesses and ladies of nobility began to pour
into the Village At The End Of The World.

It struck the residents as odd, however, that no
princess ever seemed to have a normal princess name
like Alice or Claire. These princesses all arrived with
their wrestling names: the Princessinator, Lady Doom,
Madame Fury and the curiously named, 'Princess I'm
Gonna Open Up A Can Of Whoopass!' One would
expect princesses to be wrapped in their finery:
diamonds and pearls, mink, satin and lace. These
princesses, however, had the most frightening make up
and wore their   wrestling

costumes. Some had capes, others had masks and a few carried some gruesome weapons. Of course, these would not be allowed in the ring but were more for show to intimidate the other wrestlers.

A coterie of twenty referees had been imported from the Big City to ensure that the matches were fair and unbiased. All the major television, radio and news media were there in force, ready to analyze every detail of what happened during the tournament. Bookmakers had appeared from nowhere and were already giving odds on who would win, who would lose and who would have to go to hospital. Several ambulances stood parked by the village green, ready to deal with any emergencies, along with an extensive team of doctors, nurses and paramedics. Grandpa, and his police force, maintained a strong presence around the village to make sure that no 'unofficial' matches began in the streets between the competitors.

The bookmakers had already chosen their favourites: Princess Sarah Kate (not a very scary name) was given odds of 5/2 to win. Lady Jane Destructo was a little worse off at 3/1. Baroness Hildegard von Hoffenbausenfurgenblitzenkirschfleigemenjurgenflur genmurgenwurgensen (known as Hildegard the Hammer) was dragging at 7/2 and 'The Tiara Tantrum' was the bookies' favourite at 2/1.

January 30th came, the beginning of the long
weekend and people just seemed to flood off the trains
in the Land Of The Windmills and pour along the
Village At The End Of The World Highway. In all, over
the space of three days, 24,679 people made the journey
from the Big City to watch the First Annual World
Princess Wrestling Championships. Most of them slept
on the beach. A few were lucky enough to find a bed in
the hastily constructed wooden hotels that a few
enterprising musicians had constructed. Prices were
extortionate because demand outstripped supply by a
hundred to one.

At 7:04pm exactly, 24,679 people were gathered in
the tiered seating that had been erected all around the
village green, watching what was happening in the little
wrestling ring at the centre of all the seating. In her dual
role as village herald and as a princess herself, Princess
Lydia Lion entered the ring and roared at the top of her
voice to get everyone quietened down.

"People of the Village At The End Of The World
and esteemed guests, hear ye, hear ye, hear ye. I now
declare the First Annual World Princess Wrestling
Championships open. May God bless her and all who
sail in her." With that, all one hundred and thirteen
competitors paraded into the ring, shouting and
whipping the   crowd up into a

frenzy. Some carried their weapons, some carried flags and one even led a tiger on a lead into the ring.

When the crowd saw the wrestlers, they went crazy: cheering, yelling, whooping and hollering. Mr. Hubert Q. Lion leaned back on his lion chair in the VIP box and said to himself, 'this is more like it.' The smell of hotdogs, popcorn and tiger poop was thick in the air and Mr. Hubert Q. Lion loved it.

After the opening ceremony, the crowd dispersed to the sixteen other rings around the village to watch whichever wrestling match they were interested in. Nobody would wrestle in this central ring until the final match to decide who would win the big sack of money. There was all manner of intrigue in almost every match throughout the village: people distracting the referee while their friend jumped in to the ring to inflict a little more damage, double crossing friends becoming enemies and wrestlers who hit the referee by accident, knocking him out cold. With the exception of the two symphony orchestras, everyone in the village agreed that this was much more entertaining than watching the Greatest Concert In The World.

As the contest progressed and the contenders moved past the first round, the field of wrestlers was reduced to less than half its original size. As they had a two day break to recover, just thirty two competitors remained from the original 113. Graciously, those princesses who had been defeated removed their wrestling garb and put on clothes more appropriate for a princess. They were then welcomed into the VIP enclosures at any and every match, including the final. Princess Thunder became the much more princess-like Princess Emma. Lady Laser was renamed Lady Lucia. Queen Doom became the delightful Queen Catherine of the South.

Before too long, there were just sixteen wrestlers left (which meant ninety seven proper princesses and ladies swanning around the Village At The End Of The World). Things were now becoming serious. Every match was almost a life and death situation for the contenders. Security was stepped up with four referees for each match to make sure that nobody was cheating. The massive crowd that had come to the village had, if anything, grown bigger and they were loving every minute of the wrestling.

Then it was the quarter finals: just eight wrestlers left in the competition. These matches were something special: fought inside a huge steel cage so that the competitors couldn't leave the ring. Eight referees for each match kept everything on the straight and level but even with that, there were a few attempts by wrestling princess   friends of the proper fighters who tried to interfere with the match.

The semi finals were, as the bookmakers had predicted between Princess Sarah Kate and The Tiara Tantrum, and Hildegard the Hammer and Lady Jane Destructo. The bout between Princess Sarah Kate and The Tiara Tantrum was almost a foregone conclusion: The Tiara Tantrum had been unstoppable throughout the tournament while Princess Sarah Kate had been lucky in the draw and unpredictable in her performance. Yet somehow, as The Tiara Tantrum jumped from the top rope, Princess Sarah Kate managed to move out of the way of the flying elbow. Then out of nowhere, the princess found some reserves of strength and with a stunning Vertical Suplex, she threw The Tiara Tantrum high in the air and onto the canvas. After that it was all over. The Tiara Tantrum never recovered and in wasn't long before Princess Sarah Kate had pinned her and the bell was ringing to declare Princess Sarah Kate as the winner.

The match between Hildegard the Hammer and Lady Jane Destructo was a nail biting, edge-of-the-seat affair with constant changes of fortune when either gentlewoman might have gained the upper hand. As it was, the Baroness Hildegard was the one who managed to somehow force Lady Jane Destructo into submission just as the referees were considering calling the match a draw.

Two days later came the match for third place between The Tiara Tantrum and Lady Jane Destructo. After a technically perfect but essentially boring wrestling match, Lady Jane Destructo emerged victorious, and removed her mask to reveal that she was in fact the famously beautiful Lady Jane Hallham-Smythe, heiress to the Big City Railroad Corporation fortune and well known society girl.

Finally, after a month of preparation came the big show: the final of the First Annual World Princess Wrestling Championships between Princess Sarah Kate and Baroness Hildegard von Hoffenbausenfurgenblitzenkirschfleigemenjurgenflur genmurgenwurgensen, known as Hildegard the Hammer.

Hours before the match was due to begin, the stands were full of wrestling fans eating hot dogs, pretzels, popcorn and drinking literally gallons of soda. All the sugar was making the atmosphere electric and as 6:47pm slowly rolled around the audience became more and more excited.

With a flash of fireworks and loud music, Princess Sarah Kate entered the arena from one side, flanked by a dozen princesses dressed in their most beautiful evening wear. She   herself was also dressed in a ballgown but as she reached the ring, she tore it off to reveal her wrestling outfit: a white one piece cat suit. The crowd went wild with excitement, not holding anything back.

Then the lights blacked out and the ominous music of a heel (a bad guy in wrestling) began to play. As the lights slowly raised, the baroness stood alone with an enormous hammer resting on her shoulder. With another explosion of light and music, she threw the hammer into the crowd (it turned out to be made of foam) and ran towards the ring.

There was no time for an announcer to introduce the two wrestlers. As soon as Hildegard the Hammer was in the ring, they were ready to fight. As they circled and taunted one another, the crowd were frantic with excitement. The two wrestlers tried to wear each other down with their moves: the DDT, the Flying Clothesline, the Suplex, the Crucifix, the Sunset Flip and many others. These were two ladies of nobility that were evenly matched. Princess Sarah Kate was young and fast. Hildegard the Hammer was almost twice the princess' ages but was strong as an ox and technically perfect.

At one point it seemed that Princess Sarah Kate would be the winner. The next moment, roles would be reversed and Hildegard the Hammer would have the upper hand. For what seemed like a lifetime, neither was quite able to wear the other down enough to perform a devastating finishing move. Then, Hildegard somehow managed to trick the princess. Hildegard bounced off the rope but while Princess Sarah Kate held out her arm to knock over her opponent as she bounced back, somehow Hildegard spun through the ropes and headbutted Sarah Kate in the stomach. The princess collapsed with the wind knocked out of her.

As Princess Sarah Kate lay unmoving in the middle of the ring, Hildegard the Hammer made the classic mistake of many wrestlers before she performed her finishing move. She turned to the crowd to gloat in her success. She didn't see the princess begin to stir on the ground. Hildegard climbed the turnbuckle, right to the very top rope and turned to make her flying leap that would surely win the match for her. Yet as she turned, she saw that Princess Sarah Kate was no longer lying on the canvas in the centre of the ring. She was standing right in front of Hildegard. Without any hesitation, the princess picked Hildegard up with both hands, spun her in the air and dropped her from above her head onto the canvas.

Hildegard was so surprised at what had happened that she just lay there as the princess bounced off the ropes, jumped over her once, bounced off the ropes on the other side, jumped over her again, bounced off the ropes again, jumped in the air and landed on her bum-first with a thud. Lifting her legs, the princess pinned Hildegard's shoulders to the canvas. The referee slid along the floor beside her and slapped the ground: one...two...three. Princess Sarah Kate heard the bell ringing and the voice of the announcer booming across the arena, "Ladies and gentlemen, by pinfall, the winner of the First Annual World Princess Wrestling Championships is Princess Sarah Kate."

Princess Sarah Kate was elated. Not just because of the huge sack of money that Mr. Hubert Q. Lion was now presenting her but because of what she was about to do. Ignoring the crowd and everyone else around who was congratulating her, Princess Sarah Kate found Bob and removed her mask, revealing herself to be Joy, Bob's wife.

The crowd collectively gasped as they all had the same thought: Joy isn't a princess. That means she can't compete in the World Princess Wrestling Championships. Fortunately, before the wrestling audience transformed itself into a lynch mob, Queen Catherine of the South grabbed the microphone. "It's true," she wailed, "Joy is my daughter!"

But that is another story entirely...

queen catherine of the south

The arrival of Queen Catherine of the South (or
Queen Doom to give her her wrestling pseudonym) and
her subsequent announcement threw the Village At The
End Of The World into uproar. You will recall that at
the end of the First Annual World Princess Wrestling
Championships, Princess Sarah Kate had been
victorious but before she could be awarded the big sack
of money, she had revealed herself to be none other than
Joy, wife of Bob and daughter of Wilson, the deputy
mayor. With Queen Catherine of the South's sudden
announcement that Joy was her daughter, this in turn
meant that not only was Joy a princess but that Bob was
a prince and that Wilson was a king.

With the crowd already at fever pitch from the
wrestling, Mr. Hubert Q. Lion decided that this was
definitely not the forum to seek the truth from this
family. As the until recently ranking official in the
village (technically, he too was a prince, having married

Princess Lydia), he wrapped up the wrestling tournament and somehow managed to convince the crowds to return to the Big City with the promise that next year's championship would be bigger and better.

The entertainment was over for this year and so the crowds set off along the Village At The End Of The World Highway towards the Land Of The Windmills and the railway station that would take them back home. As the dust settled, the Village At The End Of The World tried to resume normal life. The first order of business was to clean the village after all of the guests. The beach was a mess, there were half eaten hot dogs everywhere and the wrestling rings needed to be carefully dismantled and put into storage for next year. Everyone was desperate to hear what Queen Catherine of the South had to say but Mr. Hubert Q. Lion wanted the village ship-shape before they began to worry about new business. He also decided to hold onto the huge sack of money until he had heard the story, just in case.

In the space of three days, the village went from what looked like the scene of a hurricane to one of the tidiest and smartest villages in the whole world. The residents had outdone themselves in restoring their proud little village to the way it should be.

After he had conducted his final inspection, Mr. Hubert Q. Lion declared the First Annual World Princess Wrestling Championships a success. In the next sentence, he convened a village meeting. At that meeting, the entire village would decide the fate of Queen Catherine of the South, Bob (who might be a prince), Joy (who probably was a princess) and Wilson (who had a fifty-fifty chance of being a king).

The bookmakers, ever keen to make a quick buck saw the potential in this whole situation and stuck around to take bets on the outcome of the proceedings. They were giving Queen Catherine of the South odds of 4/1 to be run out of the village. Wilson was given odds of 2/1 of being stripped of his title as deputy mayor. Bob and Joy didn't fair much better: 3/1 that they would have a blazing row in front of the whole village because Joy had never told Bob that she was a princess.

The village green was transformed from a wrestling arena to what looked like a courtroom. In the dock sat the four 'accused': Bob, Joy, Wilson and Queen Catherine of the South. Mr. Hubert Q. Lion sat as judge. Grandpa and the four other monkeys kept a watchful eye as court bailiffs. For some reason, known only to themselves, a small string section had formed and were tuning up, ready to perform any incidental music that was needed.

One by one, the defendants were called to the

stand. Bob was exonerated: he knew nothing about the whole sorry situation since it had happened long before he even met Joy. Joy was similarly able to claim innocence since she had been just a baby at the time. Wilson was clearly hiding something but despite repeated questioning by Mr. Hubert Q. Lion, he was obviously not going to crack.

As Queen Catherine of the South took the stand, she began to wail before Mr. Hubert Q. Lion had a chance to ask her any questions. Her story went something like this...

Many years ago, King Wilson and Queen Catherine of the South had lived and ruled in the kingdom of the south. It was an enormous kingdom with many loyal subjects. They had been the best rulers that the kingdom had ever had and as a result, many people were attracted to live in the area. Their castle was simply enormous. The king and queen regularly found a room that they'd never been in before. That's how big their palace was. There were at least a hundred towers in the castle, but no-one had ever counted them all since they were so spread out and hidden behind one another. The only way you could have counted them all was from the air. The castle was riddled with secret

passages and hidden doorways, most of which the king
and queen knew nothing about. They were forever
finding a new tunnel that took them to a part of the
castle that they had never seen. Getting back to where
they had started was always the challenge.

If the king and queen had any weakness it was that
they were fanatical about country and western music.
Not only did they own a copy of every country and
western record that had ever been made, they employed
three permanent country and western bands to
perform in the palace. There was one in the king and
queen's private apartments, one in the kitchen where
the food was prepared and of course one in the Great
Hall to perform during the king and queen's famous
country and western banquets.

The country and western banquets were famed
throughout the land. The Great Hall was so immense
that the king and queen didn't even bother to send out
invitations: the hall was big enough to hold everyone
who happened to come along. You didn't need a ticket
to come to the banquet, merely a cowboy hat. The dress
code was incredibly strict: if you tried to get in with a
fedora or even a trilby, you would be turned away at the
door. Only stetsons and ten gallon hats were allowed.

Since nobody was entirely sure what proper
country and western food was, the king and queen more

or less served whatever they felt like serving and passed it off as genuine country and western food. The most famous dish was roasted pig, which was cooked on a spit right there over the fire in the Great Hall. The long table would be piled high with meat, vegetables, potatoes and all kinds of delicacies. The eating part alone of the evening's entertainment would last until well past midnight.

Once all of the guests were satisfied with their country and western food, the country and western dancing music began in earnest. To get people in the mood, the band played right through the feast but when the eating was done with, it was time for the dancing. They did the kind of dancing called 'line dancing' where everybody lines up and a caller at the front tells them exactly how to dance. The king and queen were experts and line dancing and all of their country and western visitors were amazed at how well both the king and queen danced, especially after eating such a huge country and western banquet.

One day, joy of joys, Queen Catherine of the South found out that she was going to have a baby. The king and queen were so happy: they would have a child to dress up in cute little country and western outfits and to teach him or her how to line dance. The castle would be filled with the life of a new child. In nine short months, the baby was born and given three names: one after each of her grandmothers and a name to show how much happiness she had brought to her mother and father: Princess Joy Sarah Kate of the South.

From the day she was born, Princess Joy was immersed in country and western music. The little radio beside her crib played it almost twenty four hours a day to soothe her. Joy was dressed in little gingham dresses and denim dungarees, always accessorized with a baby-sized cowboy hat. She was the most country and western baby in the whole kingdom.

As she grew, Princess Joy became not only the most country and western baby in the kingdom, but also one of the most curious. She wanted to look at everything, play with everything and (just like most babies) put everything in her mouth. When she learned to crawl, things became really serious: the combination of a curious baby and a castle filled with secret passageways is a dangerous combination. Queen Catherine of the South would but her baby in her playpen and return a minute later to find the child escaped through a trapdoor that nobody knew was there. Or she would be playing with some books on the shelf and accidentally find a switch that opened up a secret door that had been hidden for years.

This was, of course, wonderful small talk with their friends, "You'll never guess what Princess Joy did this morning..." It was also, however, a source of great worry to her parents. Once or twice, baby Joy had disappeared; crawling off down a secret passageway. As with most secret passageways, the door often closed automatically once you had gone through so King Wilson and Queen Catherine of the South had to first find the secret entrance before they could rescue their baby. They did their best to keep the baby safe but there were so many secret places in the castle, they simply couldn't find somewhere that was safe to put her.

Quite by chance, King Wilson found a room in the castle that was perfect as a baby room: it had a single door, bare walls, a floor with floorboards with clearly no trapdoor to be found and a single window that was covered with heavy steel bars. There was no way in or out apart from the heavy door that could be locked from the inside and the outside. This was a perfect nursery for the baby. After consulting his wife, King Wilson began turning this room into a room more suited for a baby: carpet on the floor and a new coat of paint on the walls but not before he had carefully tested every inch of the room to make sure there were no secrets.

With the new nursery, Princess

Joy's nanny could relax a little. Before, she had to literally watch the baby without blinking or she would be gone. Now, she could relax in her rocking chair that was piled high with cushions. As Princess Joy played with her toys, the nanny could do some knitting or catch up on reading her favourite magazine: Southern Belle.

Life returned to something approaching normality. King Wilson and Queen Catherine had the occasional country and western banquet and spent the rest of the time doting and cooing over their beautiful Princess Joy. The princess, for her part, explored every part of her nursery and, just like her father, was unable to find any secret passages, trapdoor or tunnels.

One rainy afternoon, as the nanny idly dozed in her rocking chair, Princess Joy happened to get her diaper caught on what looked like a loose nail in the skirting board. Before they knew what was happening, the entire floor slid away and Princess Joy and her nanny were sliding down a slippery slope in the dark. With a bump, they arrived on the ground just outside the very outer wall of the castle. The nanny, oblivious to what had happened was still sleeping and gently rocking in her chair. An almost inaudible snore escaped from her lips. Princess Joy, however, was wide awake. With a whole new woods ahead of her to explore, the princess began to crawl further and further away from the castle.

As King Wilson and Queen Catherine of the South entered the room, they were horrified to find both the baby and her nanny missing. A quick search of the room soon revealed the loose nail, the thread of nappy fabric and the secret exit. King Wilson pushed the nail and without warning, the king and queen found that they too were sliding down the slippery slope. With a bump, they landed on the ground and found the nanny still snoozing in her rocking chair.

When it became clear what had happened, all three began panicking: King Wilson, Queen Catherine of the South and the nanny. King Wilson promised that, whatever happened, he would find their daughter. He set out into the woods with his faithful hound, Caesar, and his shotgun to ward off anything that might want to harm him or his daughter. Queen Catherine of the South had returned to the castle weeping to wait for the return of her husband and the baby.

With that, Queen Catherine finished her story, since she didn't know what had happened to either King Wilson or Princess Joy after they had gone into the woods. Mr. Hubert Q. Lion demanded that Wilson return to the stand and continue the story. Reluctantly, Wilson took up the tale...

Wilson could remember none of what Queen Catherine of the South had told the courtroom. Her face was somehow familiar and he thought he could remember the name 'King Wilson' but that was all. The first thing in his life that he rememberer was waking up in the woods with an enormous headache with the only thought that he had to find his daughter. He didn't remember that he was a king or that he lived in an enormous castle with over a hundred towers. All he could think about was that he had to find his daughter.

As he looked around, Wilson saw his shotgun and his dog, Caesar and came to the conclusion that he was a hunter by profession. That didn't explain the whole daughter issue but he would sort it all out in his head once he had found her. Wilson set off for the nearest police station to see if they could help him. As luck would have it, a woodcutter had found Princess Joy crawling around in the woods and had taken her to that very same police station.

Anyway, to cut a long story short, Wilson had been so overjoyed at being reunited with his daughter that he never sat down to work out exactly who he was or why he had woken up in the woods with a headache. So he had spent the next thirty years up until now assuming that he was a hunter who had bumped his head in the village. Caesar, his faithful hound had long since died and gone to heaven but Wilson and Joy had found a little house to rent in the Big City.

Wilson had become famous as a hunter and Joy had won a very strange competition and had a symphony orchestra that followed her about. Wilson had come to the Village At The End Of The World to hunt down Mr. Hubert Q. Lion and Joy had followed to get some advice from her father. The rest is, as they say, history.

Mr. Hubert Q. Lion seemed very thoughtful and excused Wilson from the stand. Thanking both Wilson and Queen Catherine of the South for their honesty, the mayor called a recess of the court. He needed some time to think all of this through. During the recess, Wilson introduced himself properly to Queen Catherine of the South. Bob and Joy looked on knowingly: it was as if these two, who had been married before, were meeting for the first time. It was definitely love at first sight.

In just over an hour, Mr. Hubert Q. Lion returned to his seat and Grandpa, officious as ever, was saying, "All rise for Mr. Hubert Q. Lion." The mayor thanked everyone for their patience and thanked Wilson and Queen Catherine of the South for their story.

"There is," he said, "however, one thing that troubles me. Somehow, Joy knew that she was a princess. Otherwise she wouldn't have entered the First Annual World Princess Wrestling Championships. That is the only piece left missing from our puzzle. Joy, we need to hear from you one more time."

Slowly and deliberately, Joy took the stand. In her hand, she held half of a heart shaped locket on a delicate gold chain. Queen Catherine of the South recognized it instantly. "Ever since I can remember, I've had this broken locket hanging around my neck. I think I was wearing it when the woodcutter found me in the woods. I never knew what it was and despite spending hours in the Big City library, I couldn't find any information. When the wrestlers all arrived in the village for the First Annual Princess Wrestling Championships, I saw one of them wore the other half of my locket. That was Queen Doom, or Queen Catherine of the South. It was then that I knew that I was really a princess."

In floods of tears, Joy left the stand and went to hug her recently reunited family, and to introduce her husband Bob, of whom she was very proud.

As Mr. Hubert Q. Lion ruminated this new

development, he realised that now they had the truth. Hitting his gavel on the table in front of him, he pronounced the defendants not guilty. There was, however, just one more thing that needed to be cleared up while everyone was present. The Village At The End Of The World was just on the very edge of the southern kingdom and the knights of Queen Catherine of the South were well known for the white plumage they wore on their helmets. "Queen Catherine, before we wrap up these proceedings, please tell us how Baz managed to find an entire suit of armour belonging to one of your knights by the side of the road?" demanded Mr. Hubert Q. Lion.

Queen Catherine of the South looked blankly at the mayor. "I have absolutely no idea," she replied. After an awkward silence, someone in the audience cleared their throat. "Umm...I think I might know something about that"

But that is another story entirely...

the red baron

As one, the crowd turned to see who had spoken up. There, on a wooden bench about half way to the back sat Cyril the Cartographer, looking very sheepish indeed. Since this was clearly going to be another long and drawn out story, Mr. Hubert Q. Lion suggested that rather than continue the proceedings in front of the court and since no crime had been committed, it would be better to hear the whole story from start to finish over a cold glass of lemonade. As such, he invited the entire village to come to his home the following afternoon where there would be a garden party. Cyril would have the opportunity to get the story off his chest and anyone else who felt the need to unburden themselves would also be given the chance. Mr. Hubert Q. Lion was tired of secrets from the past and wanted everybody to get everything out in the open. He hoped it would foster village pride and bind the community together.

Next afternoon, shortly after lunch, the whole

village began to arrive at the Lion residence. Mr. Hubert Q. and Princess Lydia Lion were the perfect host and hostess: greeting everyone as they arrived and offering them lemonade and canapés. The people of the Village At The End Of The World had unanimously decided that this was the social event of the season and had appeared decked out in their finery and dressed in their most ostentatious summer wardrobes.

In a moment of quiet self-flattery, Cyril decided that all these people had come to hear his story. The truth of the matter was that nobody wanted to miss the opportunity to swish around in their flouncy summer dresses or to show off their special summer bonnet. And that was just the men of the village!

There were even one or two visiting dignitaries who were present. Most notably was Baron Friedrich and Baroness Hildegard von Hoffenbausenfurgenblitzenkirschfleigemenjurgenflur genmurgenwurgensen. This time, the baroness wore a garb much more appropriate for a lady of her station, rather than the wrestling outfit that they had last seen her wear. Mr. Hubert Q. Lion and Baron Friedrich were becoming the best of chums and the baron was often to be found in the environs of the village, playing a game of golf or drinking lemonade with his friend, the lion. Baroness Hildegard and Joy were becoming close too, swapping wrestling tips and crochet patterns, despite the fact that they had met as opponents in the final of the First Annual World Princess Wrestling Championships.

In the hazy afternoon sun, Princess Lydia declared it the most successful garden party she had ever hosted. Mr. Hubert Q. Lion invited everyone to find a seat in the shade as it was time for them to hear Cyril's story. If anyone else had a story they wished to tell, they should write their name on a piece of paper and pass it to the mayor who would act as Master of Ceremonies.

As the people sat down under trees and in the shade of the gooseberry bushes, Cyril took the floor and began to relate his sorry tale.

"As you all know, my name is Cyril and I'm the cartographer that drew the original map of the Village At The End Of The World and the area around it. Most of you also know that my spelling isn't that great — that's how Chihuahua ended up going into the Giant's Desert by herself. [The map had said that it was the Giant's Dessert!] As a matter of fact, it's my terrible spelling that is the basis of this whole story.

Many years ago, when I lived in the Big City, I was a

very important cartographer. That's someone who makes maps. I did all kinds of important work for the government, industry and the military. Of course, everybody knew my spelling was simply awful so, every time I finished drawing a map, it would be checked and re-checked by the experts to make sure there weren't any problems like the one we had with Chihuahua. My maps were in all of the important textbooks, ship's maprooms, and even made it into the newspaper a couple of times. I was widely believed to be the best map maker in the world. Apart from my spelling of course."

Sensing that the crowd was losing interest in this apparently dull story, Mr. Hubert Q. Lion tried to encourage Cyril to get to the point. "Yes, but what's that got to do with the suit of armour?" he said. Without really paying any attention to Mr. Hubert Q. Lion, Cyril continued with his eyes half closed...

"I used to make big money back in those days from every map that I drew. Sometimes, I would spend months trekking through the mountains or paddling along a river to make sure that my map was as perfect as it could possibly be. My maps took account of all kinds of things: magnetic north, the Mercator Projection and even things like tides and wind patterns.

Anyway, one day I got a telegram from an interesting source. I still have it, because I was so honoured to have received it."

WESTERN UNION

FAO Cyril (Cartographer) STOP
Need map urgently STOP
Sending plane to collect you STOP
Come immediately STOP
The Red Baron STOP

Although there was a look exchanged between Baron Friedrich and his wife, nobody else at the party saw it and Cyril continued with his story...

"It didn't occur to me the trouble I was about to get into. I mean, the Red Baron was one of the best known and talented land explorers of this century. Over the years, he had (according to rumour) spent more money on exploring than most kings see in a lifetime. It was

well known that those in his employ became very rich,
very quickly. To be asked to draw a map for the Red
Baron was an incredible honour, not to mention a very
quick way to retire from the proceeds.

Despite the Red Baron's considerable wealth, he
sent me a rickety old plane that was held together with
baler twine and old bits of chewing gum. Nevertheless,
when we met, he was very gracious and offered me a
substantial amount of money to draw just one map for
him. It seemed that the baron had decided to create a
treasure map, leaving clues all around the country. This
was a well planned but misguided attempt to encourage
new explorers into the profession. 'It was important,'
the baron said, 'that the map was accurate but vague.
After all, we don't want these young upstarts to find the
treasure too easily, now do we?'

The treasure that the baron was burying was quite
a substantial sum of money, even by the baron's
standards and so, there could be no mistakes in the
map. The baron had planned everything in
the most precise detail: where the
hunt would begin, what parts of the
countryside that the trail would pass
by and where the treasure would
eventually be buried. To make it easy for
me, the baron brought me the length of

the trail: a considerable distance. In all it took us seven weeks to travel from start to finish and I added to my map as we went, marking in the key features and the names of all the landmarks.

That was where the problem lay. Usually, I would have had an army of people checking my maps to make sure that my spelling was correct. This time, there was only me and the baron who was not troubled with details like that – all he wanted to do was roam about the wilderness. So I was left to pray that my spelling would, for once, be correct.

Sadly, this was not to be. Instead of the route beginning at 147 Prune Street, what I actually wrote was 147 Proon Street. A mistake which was never spotted. What made it worse was that Prune Street and Proon Street were on opposite sides of the big city. The map next called for a long trek that passed through the Finger Gorge. I wrote this as 'Fingra Gorge.' This was an even worse mistake: the Finger Gorge was due east of the city. Fingra Gorge was due west. Next, the would be explorer had to travel due north through the Valley of Figs, a beautiful place filled with fig groves with plenty of shade for the traveller. That is not, however what I wrote on his map. The Valley of Pigs is due north of the Fingra Gorge. It is not filled with pigs, however. They had all been wiped out when a mudslide had made the valley all but impassable. The mistakes on the map continued, leading the treasure hunters through increasingly more dangerous trials and eventually leading them to a lonely spot in the desert with no water within a day's journey.

Despite his thoroughness in laying the trail, the Red Baron made no attempt to check the trail that was in his head against the trail that I had drawn on the map. He had other things on his mind: he was about to try to find the end of the world. Like many explorers of his era, the Red Baron packed the strangest things for his journey: a sewing machine, fourteen barrels of passion fruits, enough salted meat to sink a battleship and a full suit of armour. He invited me to come along for the journey which I did – it would be a good experience to map some previously uncharted territory.

The treasure map was locked in a safe in the baron's castle and we set off on our journey. Two years it took us to arrive at the end of the world, and I can tell you, it was something of a let down. When we got here, we realised that we had reached the ocean. Unfortunately, despite the baron's idiosyncratic luggage, he had not packed a boat. There was no village here, just a few mango and palm trees. We hung around waiting to see what would happen and then something did: we ran out of passion fruit.

For some reason, this was a personal disaster for the Red Baron. I think they were his way of holding on to his sanity. Without warning, our little camp on the beach was broken and we set off, back towards the Big City. After a few days' traveling, the baron decided we were not moving fast enough. 'It is time,' he said, 'to shed all of this extra baggage we were carrying.' The suit of armour was cast aside at the side of the road along with most of the salted meat we were carrying. This was to be a quick march back towards home and the safety of the passion fruits that could be bought in the marketplace. When I asked him about the sewing machine, he mysteriously responded, 'NO! We must *always* carry a sewing machine.'

It must have been some kind of record, but we made it from the end of the world back to the Big City in just eighteen months, a journey that you all know takes two years normally.

It must have been a couple of months after we returned and life had settled back down again that I saw the headline in the newspaper.

The red baron has buried a reputed small fortune somewhere in the countryside and is calling for all young explorers to participate in the treasure hunt. For a copy of the map, report to 147 Proon Street this coming Monday. First to find the treasure gets to keep it.

"That following Monday, I reported to 147 Proon Street to wish the explorers well in their journey. The residents of 147 Proon Street were somewhat taken aback, since it was the residents of 147 Prune Street who had agreed to using their address as the start of the treasure hunt. However, this was all glossed over in the festival atmosphere of the day. Twenty seven young explorers, filled with dreams of greatness set off following my map which had been carefully copied. I was so proud that I shook each one of them by the hand and wished them the very best of luck.

As they days went by, however, I became more and more alarmed at the headlines in the newspapers:

★ NEWS ★
Map Send Explorers
Wrong Direction

★ NEWS ★
3 Explorers
Missing

★ NEWS ★
6 Explorers Caught
In Earthquake

"Although there was nothing I could have done about the earthquake, I couldn't help but feel partly responsible. I just knew that it was my poor spelling that had put these young people in harm's way.

The final headline worried me the most. The Red Baron was well known as an explorer but he was also well known for his ability to hold a grudge. I was in big trouble indeed. I decided that there was only one sure fire way of keeping myself safe. An explorer would never ever return to somewhere he had already discovered. After all, what was the point? I would return to the end of the world and live out my days in hiding from the Red Baron. When I had made the two year trip, I found Chihuahua's entire family already here and in hiding from their own pursuer. We made a pact never to reveal to anyone how or why we had ended up on this particular beach and why we had founded the Village At The End Of The World."

Exhausted, Cyril took a seat beneath a cherry tree that was in full blossom. Mr. Hubert Q. Lion was about to publicly thank Cyril for his confession when out of the corner of his eye, he saw a very heated discussion between the baron and baroness. Baroness Hildegard was prodding her husband in the ribs and furiously whispering something to him. As Mr. Hubert Q. Lion watched, Baron Friedrich von Hoffenbausenfurgenblitzenkirschfleigemenjurgenflur genmurgenwurgensen slowly rose to his feet with his hat in his hands, wringing it as if he was about to make a shocking confession of his own.

With his announcement that he was the Red Baron, the jaws of everyone listening dropped. "What can I say," continued Baron Friedrich, "I really love passion fruits." With that, the crowd dissolved into fits of giggles.

Now that the afternoon had taken such a light-hearted turn, some of the brass players from the Village At The End Of The World Symphony Orchestra took it upon themselves to tell the gathering a few more humorous stories and the   residents of the village spent the rest of the   afternoon laughing at the tall tales that   were told by the trumpet, trombone   and tuba players. Each one tried to outdo   the last and by sunset, the stories were   so ridiculous that people laughed the   whole way through from beginning to end.

As the garden party drew to a close and Mr. Hubert Q. and Princess Lydia Lion were thankfully saying goodbye to all their guests, a worrying thought struck the mayor. That explains the suit of armour, but what happened to all of the salted meat? But that is another story entirely...

fairy kisses

Nobody knew much about Pete or where he had come from. Many years ago, when Bob and Joy had gone one their honeymoon to the Land Of The Windmills, they had found him taking care of the windmills all by himself. Each day, he had to add two drops of oil to the machinery because, in his own words, a Land Of The Broken Windmills isn't nearly so beautiful.

Bob and Joy had managed to engineer a deal with their two symphony orchestras where one would stay in the Land Of The Windmills to rehearse and oil the windmills while the other returned to the Village At The End Of The World. This left Pete, the caretaker, free to retire and enjoy a life of luxury in the V.A.T.E.O.T.W. (Village At The End Of The World).

Pete was something of an enigma, but not enough of a mystery for anyone to inquire into how exactly he had come to be in the Land Of The Windmills in the first place. All of a sudden, however, Pete was a person who was very interesting. After all, it wasn't every day that you saw a grown man lost for words when he was kissed on the lips by a stunningly beautiful fairy. He had gone from being a guy who was around lots and liked to help people to someone whose life was filled with mystery and intrigue.

As with all small villages, gossip was often rife in the Village At The End World. Almost before Meredith, the Sunshine Princess had flown up in the air after kissing Pete, the rumour mill was already beginning to work. Women were talking behind closed doors. Old men were mulling things over. Children were laughing. Young people were watching carefully to get some tips. Overnight, everyone was talking about Pete and his mysterious presence in their village and, more importantly, why he had been snogged by a Sunshine Fairy.

The gossip reached ridiculous proportions. For something to do, Chihuahua wrote down a list of some of the more bizarre ideas that she heard in the course of the next few days.

* Pete was an alien from outer space.
* Pete was a criminal who had been banished to the Land Of The Windmills.
* Pete was trying to find the end of the world but had gotten a little bit lost.
* Pete was on the run from the police because he had robbed a bank in the Big City.
* Pete wasn't really Pete at all but another man with the same name.
* Pete used to be a tooth fairy himself but had been dishonourably discharged by the Fairy High Council for stealing some of the tooth money for himself.

It seemed like *everyone* was talking about Pete and 'that kiss!' Most of the men in the village secretly wished that this beautiful fairy had kissed them on the lips. Most of the women couldn't understand why such a gorgeous fairy would want to kiss a gnarly, old man like Pete. Finally, Pete decided that he had had enough of the whispering, giggling and blatant gossip that was going on behind his back. Ignoring the sign that said no men were allowed, Pete climbed onto the Herald's Dais on the village green and shouted at the top of his lungs, "Citizens of the Village At The End Of The World, I have had enough. If you want to hear the full story, meet me in the Land Of The Windmills and I'll do better than tell you the full story: I'll show you.

Unfortunately, because everyone was so busy gossiping, Chihuahua was the only one who heard the announcement but word spread quickly. It wasn't long before the whole village knew what was going on and in less than thirty minutes, the whole village had packed a picnic and set out along the Village At The End Of The World Highway. They were desperate to find out if he was really an alien, or what crime he had committed, or if he used to be the tooth fairy.

Pete spent a bit longer preparing his picnic and by the time he set out, the Village At The End Of The World was deserted. He travelled alone along the Village At The End Of The World Highway, turned left onto Land Of The Windmills Boulevard and trudged the two remaining miles up over the edge of the valley.

As he came over the crest of the hill, he realized that the size of the crowd was completely out of proportion to the number of people who lived in the Village At The End Of The World. Word had spread to the Big City about Pete's mysterious revelation and a vast number of layabouts, bums, unemployed persons and people with nothing better to do with their weekend had arrived on the milk train that morning to hear what Pete had to say. After all, who can resist a story about wrinkly old men and pretty young fairies?

The permanent stage that had been erected for the Greatest Concert In The World and the natural amphitheater of the valley made the perfect venue for Pete to tell his story. As Pete climbed onto the steel and wood platform that usually had a symphony orchestra performing or rehearsing, he realized how lonely it was up there by himself. As he drew breath to begin his complicated story, suddenly a burst of light shot through the sky, faster than lightning and suddenly came to a stop beside Pete on the stage. As the audience shielded their eyes, they realized that it was Meredith the Sunshine Fairy. Just like before, she planted a big, slobbery kiss on Pete's lips and then shot up in the sky again. As she did so, there was a weird rumbling noise from behind the stage but nobody could quite see what it was. Yet instead of disappearing, Meredith hovered in the air about fifty feet above the stage. As Pete was momentarily taken aback by the second kiss from Meredith, the audience heard the quiet sobs from the Sunshine Fairy, high above the ground.

Pete asked the audience for a few minutes to prepare his story. A few violinists who happened to have their violins in one of the windmills close by fetched their instruments and began a mini concert while the audience waited.

Now, if you'll remember, the stage had been erected at the very end of the valley. The two last windmills were powder blue and baby pink and after that, you went over the hill into the Giant's Desert. As the

violinists began their virtuoso performance, it was
interrupted regularly by all kinds of thunderous
banging from first the blue and then the pink windmill.

Next, to everyone's dismay, an upstairs window
opened in the pink windmill and some rather large,
empty wooden barrels came flying out of the windmill
and crashed onto the stage. Only two people in the
audience knew the significance of these barrels: Cyril
the Cartographer and Baron Friedrich von
Hoffenbausenfurgenblitzenkirschfleigemenjurgenflur
genmurgenwurgensen. The barrels were stenciled in
black paint, 'RB.' As each barrel crashed to the stage,
Meredith the Sunshine Fairy's wails became louder.

Eventually, the barrels stopped flying and Pete
reappeared on the stage. Covered with sweat from
throwing the heavy barrels, he sat down to rest while the
violinists finished the piece of music they were playing.
Then Pete climbed back on the stage to begin his story.

"A long time ago, I used to work as a porter for an
adventurer who they called the Red Baron. I used to
help him drive the donkeys and carts that carried all
his supplies. I was quite young and I had almost
forgotten about it, until Cyril told us his story. Anyway,
we stopped one day by the side of the road and, while
the Baron and his chums had a pow-wow, us porters did

what we usually do — duck behind the hedge with some of the rations that we had 'borrowed' off the wagons. Anyway, I was bursting to take a pee pee so I tossed a piece of salted meat in my mouth and nipped behind a hedge to relieve myself."

"Anyway, to cut a long story short, I got my trousers caught on some thorns which took me a little while to free myself from. Then I saw a raspberry bush which looked rather tempting so I had a few raspberries, since I hadn't eaten anything but salted meat and passion fruits since we left the Big City. It turned out that they weren't raspberries at all but singerberries, ironically named since they made you lose your voice for twenty four hours. In fact, they were the same berries that our wives gave us when they elected Princess Lydia as the Village Herald."

"When I heard the Red Baron shout that it was time to go, I turned to join our group again. Yet as I turned, my foot fell down a rabbit hole and got stuck. I wasn't hurt but I couldn't get my foot out again. I tried and tried to shout for help but I had eaten so many singerberries that not a single sound came from my mouth."

"Of course, they looked for me for a while but they couldn't find me since I was hidden behind some trees. They eventually gave up and carried on their way, back to the Big City, leaving me with my foot stuck in a rabbit hole and no voice. A day later, my foot was still stuck in the rabbit hole which made sleeping difficult I can tell you, my voice came back and I began to scream for help."

"As I was just about to lose my voice again from shouting so much, a burst of light came from the sky and landed beside me. Just like today and the other day, Meredith the Sunshine Fairy appeared and give me one of her big kisses on the lips. As she did, a strange noise came from over the hill behind me. Anyway, she helped me to free my foot. When she did, I found that the rabbits had eaten half of my boot away while it had been stuck in their hole. Then, as suddenly as she had appeared, she was gone again."

"When I got back to the road, I found all of these barrels full of salted meat just left by the side of the road. Oh, and the suit of armour that Baz used to scare away Père Jacques and Padre Diego. I decided to look around a see what I could find. Over the hill, I found this valley, which was empty apart from a solitary, baby pink windmill, turning in the breeze. It seemed like a nice place to live so I carried the barrels of meat one by one and stored them in this windmill. I remember carrying the last barrel to the windmill and then returning to collect the suit of armour but I was perplexed when I got back to the road and found the the armour had disappeared."

"So I returned to the pink windmill and began to live there, giving it two drops of oil every day to keep it working. I planted some fruit and some vegetables, began to raise some chickens and hoped that some day, someone might come along to rescue me. Yet nobody ever came, in spite of the fact that I erected a huge signpost with lights and everything. Bob and Joy were the first people to see it."

"Occasionally, as I was tending my vegetable garden or feeding the chickens, a burst of light would come from the sky and Meredith the Sunshine Fairy would appear. Every time it was the same thing: a burst of light, a kiss on the lips, a weird rumbling noise and when she was gone, there would be another windmill for me to look after."

To prove his point, Pete opened the curtains that hung at the very back of the stage and there, where there had been nothing before, stood a brand new sunflower-yellow windmill that was gently turning in the breeze. That explained the rumbling noise when Meredith had kissed Pete. Chihuahua giggled as she looked around the Land Of The Windmills. That meant that Meredith the Sunshine Fairy must have kissed Pete hundreds and hundreds of times. There were so many windmills, that they couldn't be counted which meant there had been so many kisses, they couldn't be counted.

"One day," Pete continued, "when the valley was almost filled up with windmills, Meredith the Sunshine Fairy just disappeared. She stopped appearing from the sky, she stopped giving me big, wet, slobbery kisses on the lips and the windmills stopped appearing. I never saw her again until the other day when I opened the jar and she got rid of the rainstorm for me. And when she kissed me, I heard a familiar rumbling sound. I saw the new windmill on the way into the valley: it's the dark-green one with the lime-green window frames and door."

"I think she's been crying because she's been trapped inside that jam jar for so long, in the darkness inside the farmer's satchel. She's not crying because she's sad. She's crying because she's so happy to see the sunshine again. And I think that probably..."

But before Pete could finish his sentence, Meredith the Sunshine Fairy burst from the sky again and landed beside him. She kissed him on the lips. Then she kissed

him again. And again and again and again. She was so
happy that she had found Pete again and that she could
see the sunshine too. The whole audience cheered and
cheered as Meredith the Sunshine Fairy showered Pete
with kisses. By the time she had finished, over a
hundred more windmills had appeared in the Land Of
The Windmills, spilling over the sides of the valley and
on into the Giant's Desert.

Then, with a final burst of light, Meredith the
Sunshine Fairy was gone, shooting higher and higher
into the air. Yet as the audience looked, not only was
Meredith gone, but so was Pete. The stage was empty
apart from the pile of wooden barrels marked 'RB' for
Red Baron. Pete had vanished. But that is another story
entirely...

cops and robbers

Grandpa, the old silverback of the group of monkeys and also the police chief of the V.A.T.E.O.T.W.P.D. (Village At The End Of The World Police Department) was well known as both an excellent policeman and an excellent detective. Up until now, he had a 100% record in solving every crime that had been committed in the Village At The End Of The World. As a matter of fact, most people were too scared to break the law, because they knew that with Grandpa around, there was no chance of getting away with it.

Not only that, with his four able Assistant Detectives (Big Rab, Lonely Jake, The Leaf and Fred), the Village At The End Of The World was one of the safest villages anywhere. The five monkeys were incredibly proud of their village and how they alone maintained law and order to a very high standard.

As a matter of fact, the troop of monkeys were so efficient and good at their jobs, the B.C.P.D. (Big City Police Department) had decided to send some of their detectives to be trained by Grandpa and his team. The group included the Big City Police Chief who wanted to come and see how the monkeys did it, especially with not just one, but two percussion sections close by (although there was only ever one in the village at a time). By an interesting twist of fate, it was the same police chief who had sent the monkeys to the village in the first place to get them out of his cells. A few other villages had also decided to send their police chiefs along. Some just wanted a little holiday from policing their own village. Others thought there might be some free food. Just a couple were actually interested to learn something new about policing.

A banner was erected at the entrance to the village:

welcome police chiefs of the world

In a village such as the Village At The End Of The World, something like this was sure to arouse great interest. After all, the First Annual Princess Wrestling Championships were finished and it was still several months to wait until the Greatest Concert In The World. As a tribute to the conference, a little group decided that they would all dress up as policemen to welcome the police chiefs and set about making policeman (and woman) outfits for every person in the village. They even went as far as making little baby-sized police clothes for the seventy three babies who were now approaching their first birthday.

The villagers didn't have to wait long. Within just two weeks, the policemen were due to arrive in the village. That morning, everyone put on their policeman uniform and lined both sides of the Village At The End Of The World Highway to welcome their guests. The policemen arrived on the train and walked into the village as a group, cheered on by the waiting crowds. The babies were so cute with their little hats and their plastic handcuffs, ready to arrest any criminals who might happen along. In all, a hundred sixty two policemen came to take part in the conference which, when added to the real policemen already in the village makes one hundred and sixty seven proper policemen. There were also countless 'fake' policemen — all the people who had dressed up for the occasion but were not really proper 'bobbies.'

Yet just as the policemen were crowding into the mayor's parlour to begin their meetings, a cry went up from a woman in the crowd. "My pearls, my pearls! Someone has stolen my pearls!" The crowd turned to find Baroness Hildegard dressed as a police constable but in a state of despair. She explained that they were a family heirloom, passed down by her great-great-great-grandmother and they were simply irreplaceable.

This was perfect. The visiting policemen would have the opportunity to watch Grandpa and the rest of the monkeys doing some real police work. Each one of the five primates swiftly swung in to action (no pun intended!). Lonely Jake and Fred began looking for clues. The Leaf and Big Rab rounded everyone up on the village green and began questioning them and demanding that they turn out their pockets. Those that refused were held upside down while he shook them. Grandpa directed the proceedings carefully with the air of a seasoned veteran who knew precisely what he was doing.

As sunset finally came, Lonely Jake and Fred had completed their search of the area and found no clues or evidence of any kind whatsoever. Despite having interviewed and searched the entire crowd, Lonely Jake and Big Rab had likewise come up empty handed. This was a disaster for Grandpa and the V.A.T.E.O.T.W.P.D. These visitors had come to see them because they were experts and yet they were being made to look like fools by someone who had clearly committed the perfect crime: they left no evidence and did not have the stolen goods on them when they were questioned by the police.

Things grew worse still when the next morning, messages came in from all over the village. 'Someone has stolen my diamond ring.' 'My sapphire necklace is gone.' 'I had an emerald bracelet but now it's missing.' 'My beautiful ruby earrings have disappeared.' In all, thirty two separate thefts had taken place during the night. In each case, a single piece of jewellery was missing. He had even managed to steal a diamond necklace from Princess Lydia Lion, something that made the mayor, Mr. Hubert Q. Lion, very angry indeed. Yet despite the Princess' extensive collection of jewellery, the robber had taken a single necklace from the box and left the rest untouched.

Grandpa could not handle this alone. This was a real life game of cops and robbers and the more cops he had, the better it would be. Using the extra man power that just happened to be in the village, he divided the visiting policemen into groups and sent them to check on each house that had been burgled. By lunchtime, each team had reported back to the V.A.T.E.O.T.W.P.S. (Village At The End Of The World Police Station). In each case, they said the same thing: the burglar had left no clues, whatsoever and despite varying quantities of jewellery in each house, the thief had stolen only one item and ignored the rest.

The policemen were beside themselves with confusion. How was it possible for a thief to commit thirty three separate crimes (counting Baroness Hildegard's pearls) and leave no clues for the police to find him or her. Of course, the police were certain that one person had been responsible for all of these crimes. It stood to reason that it was a well planned and well executed theft.

Since it was such a small village, and there happened to be so many policemen around, Grandpa decided that they would have to search each and every house in the village. The policemen groaned at what seemed like a mammoth task but as they stood on the village green, they realised that there really weren't that many houses in the village. Dividing into teams once again, the policemen began their laborious task. By noon on the third day, they had completed their job. Sadly, not a single house had been hiding the loot and all they had managed to do was to make the whole village angry with the police.

Grandpa was reluctantly about to admit defeat when Lonely Jake suggested that the swag may not have been hidden in a house, but rather in one of the other buildings in the village: the church, the mayor's office or even the police station itself. With renewed energy, all 167 policemen set off to search the rest of the village: opening drawers, looking under desks and into every nook and cranny that might have hidden the missing jewellery. Yet none of the buildings yielded anything other than a pair of shoes that Wilson thought he had lost many months before that were hiding behind a filing cabinet in the mayor's office.

As the policemen stood scratching their heads, ready to give up, a thought struck Big Rab. Since he was not well known for his intelligence, he ignored it but it struck him again. They had searched all the buildings that were still standing in the village but they had not searched the ruins of Père Jacques and Padre Diego's houses. The Castle Of The Brotherhood Of Perpetual Ferocity had clearly not been disturbed since Père Jacques had left: weeds were growing up through the ruins. A search found that no jewellery was hidden inside. Padre Diego's fortress however, was not so innocent. Through the long grass, someone had recently entered the remains of the Fortress Of The Brotherhood Of   Everlasting Hostility. The policemen   didn't even need to search too hard.   They just followed the tracks through   the destroyed fortress and found a little pink backpack that was filled to overflowing with all of the missing jewellery.

Finally, the case (or cases) was beginning to unravel. All the police had to do was to find the owner of the backpack and they would have their thief. Within the hour, Grandpa and his troop of monkeys had identified Chihuahua as the owner of the backpack. Despite the complaints and protestations from Baz, Victoria and Chihuahua herself, Big Rab handcuffed the young girl and carried her off to the V.A.T.E.O.T.W.C.J. (Village At The End Of The World County Jail) and locked her in a dusty cell that clearly hadn't been used for quite some time.

It was so rare for someone to commit a crime in the village, the monkeys had even stopped cleaning the jailhouse. So Chihuahua had to clean her own cell with a bucket and mop before Big Rab finally closed the heavy door and locked it. Poor Chihuahua was left alone with her thoughts and she began to cry. She knew she was innocent but there was no way that she could prove to any one of the 167 policemen that she was not guilty.

By nightfall, Chihuahua was still sobbing. The meal of chicken broth with some big chunks of crusty bread didn't make her feel any better either. Outside her cell, she could hear the guards change shifts. Big

Rab was leaving and she thought it sounded like Fred who was replacing her. Before long, she could hear the gentle snores of a sleeping monkey. With a fright, she heard a tapping sound on the other side of her cell wall. The more she listened, the more she was convinced that what she heard was a hammer and chisel. Someone was helping her to escape.

Just before daybreak, her rescuer finally managed to break through the wall with a hole big enough for Chihuahua to crawl through. As she squeezed her head, shoulders, body and finally her feet through the hole, she had to rub her eyes to make sure that she wasn't dreaming. There, on the other side of the wall were seventy three babies, all dressed in black, helping her escape from jail.

Now although this might seem rather odd, think back to one of the first things we ever found out about the Village At The End Of The World: when Chihuahua was just three months old, she could already walk, run and even swim. The people there were all very, very, strong and they rarely (if ever) got sick. At just less than a year old, these babies were perfectly capable of breaking someone out of the jail house.

With a nod from one of them, the babies melted back into the night, leaving Chihuahua to run home to tell her parents what had happened. The monkeys, however, had beaten her to it: when she walked up her garden path, they were lying in wait to re-arrest her and take her back to the jail. With even more weeping and wailing, Chihuahua was returned to an even more secure cell.

Yet that night, as the monkeys swapped shifts, Chihuahua heard the familiar sound of a hammer and chisel. The babies had returned to break her out of prison again. The pattern repeated itself: the babies disappeared, Chihuahua returned home, but this time she was not arrested by the monkeys. All the jewellery that had been returned to its owners was once again missing. The same exact pieces of jewellery as before. Chihuahua couldn't possibly have done it since she was in prison until moments before dawn.

By mid morning, however, Lonely Jake and Big Rab arrived at Chihuahua's front door to arrest her. No reason was given, despite the heated debate from Baz and Victoria, Chihuahua's parents. Big Rab returned her to her cell and winked at her. "Don't worry," he said, "we know you didn't do it this time. We just want you to help us catch the real thief."

Nightfall came and Chihuahua heard the comforting sound of the hammer and chisel on the outside of her cell wall. Yet this time, as she pulled herself out through the hole that the babies had opened, she could feel that something wasn't quite right. However, the babies hadn't noticed anything. As the same baby gave the nod that their job was done, suddenly the area was flooded in light. One hundred and sixty seven policemen were shining there torches at the babies, along with a couple of super bright police search lights.

In confusion and panic, the babies tried to run for it but seventy three babies are no match for 167 burly policemen. In less than a minute, the babies had been rounded up and carried to the V.A.T.E.O.T.W.P.S. For questioning. Strangely, every single baby needed their nappy changed. They all stank! It took a little while for the policemen to pluck up the courage to change the babies but when they did, they found every single piece of jewellery that was missing, hidden inside the babies' nappies.

The babies were all sentenced to a hundred days in prison for their crimes against the village and Chihuahua was exonerated. Despite their amazement at how Grandpa had solved this crime, the rest of the policemen decided that   the babies were too cute to be put in   prison. Instead, they ordered them   to be good boys and girls for the rest of   their life and to always love their mummies and daddies. Grandpa, on the other hand, was given three awards:

The Robert Peel award for police work of the highest standard, the Victoria Cross for service over and above the call of duty and the Mother's Pride Award for changing the most nappies in an hour!

the bell at the end of the world at the end of the world

It seems like there's not much else that could happen in this little collection of stories from the Village At The End Of The World. We've had the battle between Père Jacques and Padre Diego, the love story between Pete and Meredith the Sunshine Fairy and the cows (and lions) that have gotten sick and then well again.

We even know how every single person arrived in the village. Chihuahua and her entire family were hiding from the multiple Dr. Ebenezer Finkelbottoms. Cyril was on the run from the Red Baron. Mr. Hubert Q. Lion was tricked by Princess Lydia (and her butterflies) who later came to the village as his wife. Wilson came to hunt down Mr. Hubert Q. Lion but things somehow went wrong and he became the deputy mayor. The ants had come to eat the apple cores that Wilson threw out the window every day. Joy had arrived with a symphony orchestra in tow to find her father. Bob had arrived along with another symphony orchestra to find Joy. Grandpa, Lonely Jake, Big Rab, The Leaf and Fred had been sent from the Big City as the V.A.T.E.O.T.W.P.D. (Village At The End Of The World Police Department). Pete used used to work for the Red Baron and was also the caretaker of the Land Of The Windmills but had retired from that position at Bob and Joy's insistence. Queen Catherine Of The South had come to compete in the First Annual World Princess Wrestling Championships and when she had found her husband and daughter, she had never left. Lastly, Fiona and Sania had simply drifted past on a floating island one day.

That all made for an interesting and eclectic group of residents. However, there was one person who remained a mystery to one and all. His only contribution to village life was as the musical director of the Village At The End Of The World Amateur Dramatic Society. But maybe you can remember that back in the dim and distant past, just before Bob wed his wife Joy and Mr. Hubert Q. Lion married Princess Lydia, there was something of a crisis in the village. There had been no church in which to get married. Of course, the church had quickly been built but bells were the big problem.

Anyway, to cut a long story short, Deaf Al the bell maker came to the village on a deal. The old man was stone deaf from testing all of the bells that he had made. The deal was that if he made the bells for the church, Baz would make him a new hearing aid. Everything had run perfectly smoothly: the bellmaker had forged the seventeen bells that now hung in the church tower. In return, Baz had made a hearing aid for the bellmaker.

However, rather than return to his life in the Big City, Deaf Al had decided to remain in the Village At The End Of The World. After his part in the nativity play, he started to act rather strangely. To be fair, nobody in the village noticed that he was acting strangely. As a matter of fact, they thought he had gone back to the city on the milk train, since they never saw him. It was only the insomniacs that knew the man was still around. He wasn't interesting enough to gossip about, so they didn't even tell the people who were lucky enough to sleep right through the night. At least, to begin with he wasn't that interesting...

Usually, if someone couldn't sleep, they went for a walk to the beach. Often, in the dead of night, they would see Deaf Al there, pacing up and down the beach.

It was almost as if he was measuring it. Thinking nothing of it, they were more worried about going back home to a warm cup of cocoa and hopefully falling asleep in their beds.

As time went by, however, the Deaf Al became more mysterious. He seemed more purposeful in his pacing up and down the beach. It was almost as if he was measuring something out on the ground.

One night, when everyone was tucked up safely in their beds, he placed four red flags in an enormous square on the beach. He carefully hammered them into the soft sand and then promptly disappeared. A few minutes later, he reappeared from behind a sand dune with a child's plastic shovel in one hand and a green flag in the other. He paced out the distances twice, to make sure he was right then he hammered the green flag into the exact centre of the square. Furiously, he began digging a deep trench in a circle around each of the five flags. Every two minutes or so, he would look up at the waves that were breaking closer and closer the the two flags on one side of the square.

All this went unobserved by the whole village. By some coincidence, tonight was a night when everyone was sleeping. Yet what happened next woke the whole village, the sound of a monstrous machine with gears and cogs turning and clicking, motors whirring and levers and chains clanking and shuddering.

As the first waves reached the flags, the water began to spill into the trenches around the flags that were closest to the water line. Slowly at first, the little island of sand that surrounded each flag began to turn. As they turned, they rose higher, first slowly and then as more water sloshed into the trenches they rotated faster and faster until they were spinning around and around and whizzing up in the air. That is, four of the little islands spun and rose up in the air. The green flag remained on the ground; it hadn't moved an inch.

Four red flags in a perfect square were now fluttering in the breeze, two hundred feet in the air, on the top of four monstrous metal pillars festooned with seaweed and driftwood. Huge steel cables swung from the top of each pillar to the ground. Without a moment to lose, the bellmaker took his plastic shovel and began his next task. He ripped the green flag from the ground and threw it away. Next, he began to dig where it had been planted, a job that took only a few minutes. It wasn't long before his plastic spade scraped against something hard and metallic. With a gleam in his eye, Deaf Al excavated a very solid looking metal ring that was firmly anchored to the sand.

The waves were already coming close and Deaf Al

knew that he hadn't a moment to lose. He jumped
through the waves to the first two pillars that already
had waves lapping at their bases. With a supreme effort,
he dragged the chains one by one and attached them to
the ring that was buried where the green flag had been.
Then he did the same for the two pillars that were
further up the beach, and still on dry land. With all
four chains securely attached, he sank to his knees and
enjoyed the waves washing over him for a moment.

By now, most of the village was gathered at the top
of the beach, mystified as to what was going on. They
were, it has to be said, a little annoyed that Deaf Al's
antics had woken them from their slumbers but they all
wanted to find out what exactly was going on. With a
flourish, he stood up from the water, opened a little
panel on one of the pillars and pushed the green button
that was hidden inside.

If the noise had been loud before, it was positively
deafening now. Motors ground as they took the strain
on the four cables and, ever so slowly, the whole beach
began to shift. Children screamed, ladies fainted and
men scratched their heads, wondering what this could
all mean. As the   cables lifted
whatever this was   out from under the
beach, a gasp of awe   went around the
onlookers as they   realised what it was.

This was by far the biggest bell that any one of them had ever seen and probably the biggest bell in the world.

It seemed to take forever but the bell was eventually lifted clear of the beach and hung, suspended on the huge chains high in the air. Sand, water, seaweed and a few crabs fell from its edges as it rose and then it hung there, gleaming, above the bellmaker and the onlookers. From edge to edge, it had to be fifty feet and even longer from top to bottom.

The edge of the bell was just low enough for someone to touch it. It was so shiny, you could see your own reflection there, although since the bell wasn't flat, your reflection looked rather strange. Deaf Al fetched a huge hammer that he was obviously going to use to ring the bell. The head of the hammer was bigger than a man's head. The handle was about as big as a person. It was so big that Deaf Al struggled to lift it. As he swung back to strike the bell, the silence that had descended on the crowd was broken by a bloodcurdling sound:

RRROOOOAAAAARRR!!!!!!!! STOP...RIGHT...THERE!!!

Mr. Hubert Q. Lion stood at the top of the beach, silhouetted against the full moon. Deaf Al had already

beğun his swinğ to strike the bell but the lion's roar
friğhtened him so much that he missed completely, let
ğo of the hammer (which flew across the beach and
stopped ağainst a rock), spun around and fell on his
bum. In just three bounds, Mr. Hubert Q. Lion was
beside Deaf Al demandinğ to know what was ğoinğ on.
The mayor refused to let the bellmaker rinğ the bell
until he had a full explanation of what exactly was
ğoinğ on, especially since very few people realised that
Deaf Al was still livinğ in the villağe.

Without a word, Deaf Al motioned for Mr. Hubert
Q. Lion to follow him. Not wantinğ to miss what was
ğoinğ on, the rest of the villağers followed at a safe
distance, craninğ their ears to hear what the bellmaker
and the lion were talkinğ about. Grandpa and his
police force of monkeys were left to ğuard the bell and
to make sure that nobody ranğ it.

Mr. Hubert Q. Lion was constantly askinğ Deaf Al
questions but the man refused to answer him. He led
Mr. Hubert Q. Lion to a part of the beach where he had
never been before. Tucked between two sand dunes,
almost completely hidden from view, was a stone cave
that was clearly very old. Deaf Al and
the mayor entered the cave alone
while the rest of the village listened at the
entrance. In the dim light that was turned

green by all the elephant grass that covered the entrance, Deaf Al pointed to one wall of the cave. There, in paint that looked to be at least a thousand years old was a series of pictures. It didn't take Mr. Hubert Q. Lion long to realise that these were the instructions of how to raise the giant bell out of the beach. The flags, the trenches, the chains and the button were all drawn in painstaking detail.

There was, however, one thing that worried Mr. Hubert Q. Lion. There were clearly six panels marked out on the wall for the instructions yet only five had been completed. The fifth showed the green button that Deaf Al had pressed to pull the bell out of the sand. In the sixth panel, there were a couple of charcoal markings that were almost worn away. Whoever had painted these instructions had never finished them.

In a hoarse whisper, Deaf Al finally spoke. "I found these paintings a couple of weeks ago. It took me a while to work out what they meant but then I realised what they were. The people who lived in the Village At The End Of The World hundreds of years ago must have built it. I don't know why they hid it in the sand, but I'm a bellmaker so I thought I'd test it out, see what it sounded like. I don't think it's ever been rung before."

Mr. Hubert Q. Lion was nervous. The charcoal marks in the sixth panel looked like people who were running and screaming. Maybe ringing the bell would be something terrible. The mayor managed to convince Deaf Al of his ideas and they decided that the best thing would be to return to the beach, and try to operate the machine in reverse to once again bury the bell beneath the sand.

However, when they arrived at the beach, they found Grandpa losing control of the four other monkeys. Big Rab and The Leaf were climbing up and down the bell having races. Fred and Lonely Jake were fighting over the huge hammer that had been in Deaf Al's hands less than an hour ago. Before they could intervene, Lonely Jake wrestled Fred to the ground, raised the hammer high above his head and brought it down with a dull thud on the edge of the bell.

Fred, who had fallen on the ground inside the bell looked up and saw some words that he thought didn't make much sense: 'The Bell At The End Of The World At The End Of The World.' Yet, as he continued to read the inscription, his smile turned to a frown...

This bell is to mark two things: the end of the world and the end of the world. Firstly, it has been placed at the end of the world (ie the place). Secondly, when it is rung, it will mark the end of the world (the time). Grave danger faces the man who rings this bell for it will be his fault that the world is about to end.

But that isn't just a whole other story. It's a whole other book...